BRUTES

"The mystery and the danger of being a girl, of feeling crazy and vulnerable and wild, wanting to run away and be someone—anyone—is captured here across a landscape of nail polish and fire and sex, a sinister lake and the pink sky of Florida. *Brutes* is a beautiful and deeply strange novel, full of dread and longing. I loved it."
—Mariana Enríquez, author of *Our Share of the Night* and *Things We Lost in the Fire*

"Polyphonically technicolor and lushly textured, Brutes is a defiant elegy to the myth of girlhood innocence. Dizz Tate's talent is brazen—and brilliant."
—Sophie Mackintosh, author of *The Water Cure*

"Innovative, urgent, and endlessly lush, *Brutes* is the rapturous story of darkly shifting allegiances among a group of obsessive teenage girls. A masterful sentence maker, Tate is a startling and singular new voice, and her debut novel is so taut and intense it might just catch fire."
—Kimberly King Parsons, author of *Black Light*

"In the tradition of Southern Gothic literature made new, *Brutes* is dark, unsettling, lyrical, and threaded with comic moments. Set in a small and dreary Florida town, this inventive novel chronicles the collective lives of a group of girls on the precipice of adulthood and the inevitable, sorrowful surprises that come later. A mystery, the ominous disappearance of an older girl, renders the story a page-turner, but the complex characters, sharp details, insights, and lush prose are to be lingered over. Dizz Tate's debut novel is compelling and memorable."

—Binnie Kirshenbaum, author of
Hester Among the Ruins and *Rabbits for Food*

"Assured, insightful, quietly savage, Dizz Tate is capable of conjuring a whole world."

—Nicole Flattery, author of *Show Them a Good Time*

"The many voices of *Brutes* tell the reader seductive, dangerous stories about the lives of girls and women in Florida. Lyrical, propulsive, and at times savagely funny, this is an impressive debut by Dizz Tate, and it sucked me in from start to finish."

—Alix Ohlin, author of *We Want What We Want*

BRUTES

BRUTES

A NOVEL

DIZZ TATE

CATAPULT

NEW YORK

First Catapult edition: 2023

ISBN: 978-1-64622-167-7

Library of Congress Control Number: 2022944557

Jacket design by Nicole Caputo
Jacket image © Alexandra Bochkareva / Trevillion Images
Book design by Wah-Ming Chang

Catapult
New York, NY
books.catapult.co

Printed in the United States of America

1 3 5 7 9 10 8 6 4 2

We dug a hole. Our white hair warmed around the
thing, we asked, is this a genesis?
No, we agreed, the thing was not a genesis. A genesis
is when he sweeps across the water.
We nodded. It rustled. We stood closer to each other,
we asked, what is this, a stillness?
We watched it from a distance, we agreed, the thing
was not a stillness.

SABRINA ORAH MARK

Where is she?"

We imagine her mother asking first. She will say it once, quietly, standing in Sammy's bedroom doorway. She will see the flat bed. The quivering screen, ripped back from the window. The second time she asks, her voice will shake, and the third time it will rise and turn ragged.

Her father will run to the room and he will ask the question, too. "Where is she?" At first, his voice will be small, like our little sisters' voices when they come to crawl into our beds, when their dreams will not let them loose. The second time he asks, it will be demanding, like the room is a person refusing to tell him what it knows. The third time he will be on the phone, and his voice will have settled into the one he uses to preach in church, a respectful voice, a calm voice, even when he describes the devil and all the details of hell.

The question will spread through the phone lines and cause men to move from their chairs and into their cars.

Sammy's mother will call her mother, and the women she trusts around town, and though they will not repeat the question back to her, they will hang up and call others, or they will even run and knock on neighbors' doors because the question is impatient, it cannot wait for the whining of rings. We imagine the question rippling out of Sammy's house, out of Falls Landing, leaking onto the highway, over the ruins of the construction site, spreading up our apartment towers. Even the lake seems to bristle, the question tickling its surface as it moves like a first, threatening wind.

Night stains the sky slowly, then all at once.

We watch like we have always watched.

Soon we see the blue streaks of sirens. Cop cars wind down the highway, one after the other. We watch them twirl down the exit ramp and speed around the right shore of the lake. They thread through the Falls Landing gate and disappear. We can see the roof of Sammy's house beyond the white walls, strobing from darkness to blue, darkness to blue. We imagine the cops moving toward her door, their heavy hands knocking, and the twisted faces of her parents as her mother clutches her father, and her father clutches the frame of the door. We imagine the neighbors' children waking to see alien illuminations on their bedroom walls, blue messages that seem to summon their parents, who rush to check that the children are safely breathing in their beds.

Our hands shiver and our binoculars shake. We force ourselves to focus.

Figures begin to drift out of the Falls Landing gate. Some are alone, others huddle in groups. They are not women we know, but we recognize them, like women we have seen in the background of movies, or our dreams. They are built for church, in skorts and pastel-colored sweaters.

They have flashlights strapped to their foreheads so we cannot make out their features. Their faces are circles of light, like unfinished pictures. They march across the construction site and toward the lake as though they plan to conquer it. Some scrape at the dirt with long metal poles. Others have shovels and pitchforks. They poke and stab and spike our ground. They walk as far as the lip of the lake, and some hold their instruments above its surface, but we are satisfied that not one of them dares to disturb the stillness of the water. The lake is dark, indivisible from the low, starless sky, illuminated occasionally by the theme parks' swerving spotlights. A small moon leaks across the water, vague as a pool light.

We track the paths of the women. They do not hesitate, they walk smoothly. They do not seem afraid and we resent this in strangers. They cluster on the construction site, prying up the foundations of the unbuilt houses, peering under forgotten tarps and rotting planks and pallets. They knock their way into the single finished show home, their noses wrinkled, their flashlight beams passing swiftly across the needles, the wine bottles, the stained mattress. Since the roof blew off in a hurricane and the workers left, the show home is a well-known place for love. After it was abandoned, someone dragged in a mattress and strung a tent above it with jumper cables to protect it from the rain. The tent is thin and we have looked down on the shapes and shadows of bodies meeting there for years, watching as they come together and peel apart. Like guardian angels, we watch politely from our windows, but the searching women do not seem to want to bless the place. There is judgment in every move they make. They scrape the surfaces with their flashlight beams, find nothing, and leave the door rudely open.

Two women march farther, keeping to the lake's edge, past our apartments and toward the wild place, the place even we do not dare to go. We swing our binoculars to the left to follow them. The round glare of a flashlight reveals the warning sign on the wire fence that surrounds the wild place lot, the electrocuted man with crosses for eyes and sparks for hair. The tall grass beyond the fence is thick as a wall. We watch one of the women lick her thumb and test a diamond of wire. Her hand jerks. We laugh silently. We can almost see the electric jolt minnow its way through her big, disbelieving bones.

Their search is determined and choreographed, and watching them, it is like we can hear their thoughts, loud as a chant. Where is she? Where is she? Where is she? They are toneless and militant and sure.

We track the women carefully, but soon the night closes around so tightly that we begin to lose them. We chase their flashlights. In the quick, lit circles, we see a stray cat baring its teeth, the end of a snake tail, the glint of Eddie's abandoned ladder, but the scene is like a dark screen with the occasional burst of clear pixels.

We resist sleep but it tugs our eyes down, the same

way it does when we vow to stay up all night at sleepovers, but coffee and scary movies just give us stomach aches and strange dreams. We sit cross-legged at our windows, our heavy heads slumped against the glass. The action starts to skew. The bright, faceless women rise into the air like space walkers. Ladders hang loose, caught on the fabric of the sky. The women leap up to grab the rungs. They open their mouths as if to speak to us, but we only hear the screeching of the stray cats, fighting their nightly battles between our apartment blocks.

When we wake up, the sun has just appeared, a thick red muscle bleeding low across the lake. We rub our eyes and stare. The women have returned to the ground. The hot air blurs around them. They seem deflated and move slowly through the morning's pink haze. They have abandoned their instruments and seem to be calling her name over and over. They look desperate, their determination lost. We giggle. We focus our binoculars on their mouths, the lowering and widening of their pleading jaws. "Sam-my, Sam-my, Sam-my." We can hear more sirens on the highway, and the faint noise of tourists let loose from the hotels and into the theme parks across the lake.

Our mothers lean over us in our beds, and we let our eyes flutter beneath their cool hands. We like the smell of their hangovers, the tang of liquor and limes.

"Something's happened," they say.

"What?" we whisper.

"The preacher's daughter. That little girlfriend of Eddie's. They can't find her."

We keep our eyes closed. Little girlfriend. We roll our eyes behind our lids.

"The one with the short hair. What's her name?"

The one with the short hair! Our mothers are so innocent. They don't know anything about our fierce attachments, our hatching hearts.

"Sammy," we say. We try to keep our voices still.

"We've made coffee," they say.

"We'll explain everything," they say.

We nod and wait for them to leave us alone.

We return to our windows as soon as the door clicks shut behind them. The construction site below has transformed into a carnival. Tents have been raised up around the show home. Plastic trash buckets full of ice and bottled water are positioned along the Falls Landing wall. Trucks are parked up along the road to the highway, their beds a tangle of metal detectors, walking sticks, paper, and tape. The women remain, not as many as we thought, only a dozen or so, new pink t-shirts donned as a uniform. They look bright and shapeless, sprung from a multipack. They squat in front of the flaps of their tents, warming coffee over campfires or brushing their teeth, rinsing and spitting over distressed grass. We see the sheriff parked up by the Falls

Landing gate, clutching his hand radio like a kid told to stay in the corner. Even through the glass of our windows, we can hear faint voices we recognize, voices from other apartments, our mothers and grandmothers on the balconies. Some balance phones to their ears with one shoulder, a trick they learned when we were babies and always wanted to be held. Some shout across to their neighbors. We can't make out the words but we know they are saying, "Where is she?" Or they are using other words but this is what they mean. We know which mothers are praying, which mothers are offering dirty explanations, which mothers are already crying, which mothers are asking too many questions. We know every type of mother.

We go into our kitchens, the linoleum-lined corners that set off the kitchens from the brown carpet of the main rooms. We pour our coffee from the pot. We add French vanilla creamer. Three sugars. The television plays in the background on mute. We see the usual stories, the nightly fires that have been set around town all summer, small enough that they burn themselves out, leaving only smashed glass and scorch marks. The workers are still striking outside the ringed fence of the fertilizer factory, slouched on crates, angel wings of sweat sprouting between their shoulder blades. They show pictures of the little girl who got her leg chewed off by an alligator near the golf course lake, some new footage of her mother taking selfies minutes before. Then a photo of Sammy appears, a recent photograph with her shaved head, a new piercing large in the whorl of her left ear. The word *breaking* appears at the bottom of the screen, and the anchors shuffle their papers faster. Then there is a shot of her father at one of his rallies, his large hands pressed together and raised.

Our mothers reach over and extinguish the screen.

We sit and signal for them to begin.

"We don't know all the details," they say. "Still daylight and she was gone. Nothing taken with her, everything exactly the same except the screen was torn in her bedroom window."

We nod, blow on our coffee. We understand what our mothers are saying. Sometimes when we wait for them to pay in the grocery store, we leave them and look at the notice board, with all the posters of missing people. Some have been gone for years. We look at the kids from every county, their sticky smiles and their parents' pleas. We pay particular attention to the girls. They look so familiar, and yet they have gone to a place our mothers will never describe to us. We do our own research, and we hear stories full of dirt, stories that make us nauseous, though somehow we also know them, we have just been told them by our mothers using different words. We realize the woods are not woods, and the wolves are not wolves. In these stories, the ones that once sent us to sleep, the mothers are always banished or cursed or dead.

"Are you okay?" our mothers ask. "The whole town's out looking for her, so don't worry."

We look at them.

"Don't let your minds run away with you," they say. "She probably just went for a sleepover."

They bare their teeth at us. Their teeth are the color of our coffee, from an alternating diet of cigarettes and tooth whitening strips.

We dress carefully. We want to look our best but we don't want anyone to notice our efforts. We want to look lazy and gorgeous and innocent. Our beds are smothered by our discarded outfits.

Leila wears her gym shorts and one of the black hoodies her dad left behind. Britney wears a baby-blue polo shirt, butterfly clips in her hair, and a pair of white denim shorts we all want. Jody wears flip-flops with rhinestones glued onto the bands. Hazel wears Jody's old red swimsuit tucked into her shorts, stuffed with tissue to make it tight. Isabel wears a peasant skirt and a long string of plastic pearls. Christian wears a pinstriped vest and eyeliner he applies three times. We stare hard at ourselves in the mirror. Sammy is gone, we think, and our faces do not falter. We give nothing away.

We smear eye shadow up to our eyebrows. We color and shine our lips with gloss. We smile. We shimmer. We feel like we do not exist.

We find one another outside and slow down to escape our mothers. We hover behind them and walk around the lake. Eddie's ladder lies in the grass near the dock. We hopscotch between each square of it, the same way we step on every crack in the sidewalk.

"My mom says she's probably just testing her mom."

"My mom says if they don't find her, then no one has a shot in hell."

"My mom thinks it's weird her dad's calling her an angel on the news, like it makes it sound like she's dead."

We laugh at that one. Dead!

We only think about death when we think about Britney's dad.

We are careful never to think about Britney's dad.

Leila's stolen a pack of her mother's cigarettes, the kind we like the most with the silver band around the end. We crouch on the steps of the show home, Leila on the top step, the rest of us huddled below her like a human pyramid. Leila reaches behind her and slams the door firmly shut.

"Got a pen?" she says.

We empty our pockets. We only have Christian's eyeliner. Leila writes KEEP OUT on the door with a little heart.

She returns the eyeliner. Christian looks at it sadly before stuffing it into his back jeans pocket.

"We'll split up," says Leila. "We'll split up and listen to everyone."

We shrug and nod and chew on our cigarettes. We don't like to split up. We like to stay close, link arms, nod our heads on one another's shoulders, lie across one another's laps. But we do what Leila tells us to.

We walk around. We hover near clusters of women. Younger kids are glitter gluing angel wings onto the backs of pink t-shirts emblazoned with Sammy's face. There are posters stuck on every telephone pole, blanketing the show home's flimsy frame, hyphenated along the white wall. They are using an old photo of Sammy, a different one than from the news. Her hair is long and her teeth are unbraced. It is like everyone is looking for a different Sammy than the girl we watch on the wall, flying down the ladder to meet Eddie every night.

Poles and black lights and shovels wink in the white sunlight. Everything looks illuminated from the inside. Our heads hurt.

"Please do not share evidence," a church woman shouts over a megaphone. "Give it to us and it will be passed on to the correct authorities."

"Did she say *titties*?" says a boy. Another boy snorts and a woman hits their heads with a rolled-up poster.

We keep glancing back at the lake, but it is still as

always. The lake never moves, but we find its stillness hard to believe. It seems to be tricking us, and we swear if we look quickly enough just once we will catch it, squish the truth it is hiding like a fly in our fists. Across the water, the fertilizer factory bruises the sky with smoke. An orange-and-blue roller coaster releases a round of screaming hostages. The billboard for the Arabian Nights Dinner Show Experience glitters in the light, the two belly dancers undulating around the mantra of KIDS EAT FREE.

Our mothers stand a little way off, smoking and attracting dirty looks. We check in from time to time, nuzzling into their armpits. They smell sweet now, liquor edged with bodywash. They always buy us the strongest scents for the shower. Tangerine. Zesty Lime. Vanilla Brown Sugar.

"Something must be up. They wouldn't get this crowd out for nothing."

"She climbed out the window yesterday?"

"You're kidding me."

"Our girls wouldn't get these numbers."

"Well, you didn't marry a preacher."

"You can say that again."

They laugh, and then pretend to cough when the church women stare at them.

"Hey, we came to help like everybody else," they whisper. They scatter to cleave the earth with the heels of their wedge sandals.

Someone brings out a coffee urn and sets it up on a plastic table. Someone else brings beer. We can see the brown and green glass poking out between the bottles of water in the trash cans. We steal one and regroup by the show home steps. We like beer, especially when it's cold. Britney belches beautifully and we laugh.

We can hear the women's voices easily. No one is whispering anymore. The search is starting to seem like any other party. No one has found anything.

"You think she ran off?"

"Girls do, especially her age."

"Girls get taken, too."

"Don't say that."

"You know this girl shaved her hair off with her dad's razor?"

"You think he had something to do with it?"

"They do make her wear that wetsuit around the pool."

"Why?"

"Scared of her showing skin."

"I'd put my girl in a wetsuit if I thought she'd fit in one."

"You'd get a cat in easier."

"And less scratches!"

"Maybe she got spooked because of the audition?"

"What about that pretty boyfriend of hers?"

"He says he doesn't know anything."

"You trust him?"

"You think she ran off?"

"Girls do, especially her age."

We hear them sucking their iced coffee through their straws, pulling down swallows of beer. The sun seems to wipe their brains clean so they can start all over again. We finish the beer and Britney throws the bottle through the show home's empty window frame. It hits the back wall and smashes all over the mattress.

"Brit," says Leila, "that's not cool. People make love there."

Britney bites her thumbnail. Some of us giggle and some of us shake our heads, but we do not like to disagree so we forget it. We peer around the walls of the show home. Kids from the apartments get dragged along by their mothers, told to quit asking questions and just look. The smaller kids look crazy with the summer's heat, their hair matted and alive. Older kids stand around, snapping gum, still and bored as cows. Someone's gone to the big store to get snacks. We know the plastic dome containers, the sandwiches, the pale sprinkle cookies. There are a couple of rotisserie chickens to tear apart. A boy offers a girl the end of a bag of chips, and she tips her neck back to let the crumbs rain down her throat. Mothers chew, their faces softening. Boys take huge bites and girls nibble. Little kids dissect sandwiches suspiciously for things they have decided not to like. We see mouths, mouths, and more mouths, chewing orange chicken, turkey mayonnaise, refrigerated brownie bites. Saliva curls between lips. Seeds burst in simultaneous blasts from rounds of tomatoes. Veins of fat swing loose. Wisps of lettuce hang limp. Mysterious specks burrow between large white teeth.

We look at each other. "Nothing," says Leila. "They've got nothing."

"Like always," says Britney, and this time we all laugh.

2

The first time we really noticed Sammy Liu-Lou was one year ago. She started eighth grade when we started seventh. We did not know much about her then, only that she lived in one of the big white houses on the other side of the wall around Falls Landing. We knew her dad was a famous TV preacher who traveled the world doing revivals. Sometimes he spoke at our church on Sunday, and we noticed Sammy and her mother sitting in the front row, their long, dark hair hanging in sheets over their faces, their hands clasped tight. When Sammy's dad preached, especially after we failed a school eye test or had diarrhea, our mothers made us go up at the end to let him rest his big hands on either side of our heads, like he was trying to squeeze something out of us. We submitted to this, and sometimes Britney pretended to faint or talk in tongues, but we did not find it very interesting. We didn't care about men, and we didn't believe in miracles. We always thought Sammy was weird, but in a way we understood. She wore big sweaters and ate her lunch alone in the library, and once she'd yelled at a gang of girls at lunch for saying, "Oh my god." Her voice was high and squeaky as she told them to stop using God's name in vain, taut with belief. We all thought she'd cry when everyone laughed at her but she didn't. She stared at the girl who said it, and for a second the cafeteria was silent, almost afraid. We swore she seemed about to levitate. Then the bell rang, and she returned to being invisible, ignored. We forgot about her completely.

But then she had a birthday party.

She was turning fourteen, too old to invite her whole class to a birthday party, but Sammy invited every girl in the grade. She was indiscriminate. No one was left out for the fun of it. She spent a whole day handing out invitations, threw one down on every girl's desk, scattered them like dollars in a music video, flung them across her table in the cafeteria. Later that night, we gathered at the apartment's playground and listened to the eighth-grade girls as they sat around on the slide, throwing Sammy's invitations in the air and shouting, "Girls only," in an impression of her squeaky voice.

"Who does she think she is, anyway?"

"I don't even wanna go if there's no guys."

"*Girls only!*"

"You know she's got warts in her throat?"

"Her vocal cords."

"Whatever."

"She sounds like a freaking dog toy."

"She has to get them shaved off every three years with a laser."

"How do you know?"

"I asked her!"

"You just asked her?"

"That's so mean!"

"You're crazy."

The girls laughed, but we liked Sammy's voice, the crackle that made it sound like she was telling secrets no matter what she said. We couldn't wait any longer.

"Let us see it! Let us see it!" we pleaded.

The girls rolled their eyes and passed us their invitations. The paper in our palms was warm and thick, like cream cheese frosting. We unraveled the invitations and specks of paper confetti fell out. We caught them on the pads of our fingers. We squinted and saw they were in the shape of little birds.

"Let's burn them," said Kayla, Leila's big sister. She loved to burn anything, especially beautiful things. She liked to watch cheap earrings curl on the sidewalk, pink bougainvillea flowers from the pool shrink and blacken, the ends of her prettiest friend's hair vanish. We immediately put the tiny perfect birds on our tongues to save them. They dissolved like sugar paper. They even tasted sweet. The big girls made a small fire of their invitations and dared each other to stamp it out with bare feet. Leila was the first one to try but she cried when the soles of her feet met the flames.

Still, on the day of the party they were all lined up. Every eighth-grade girl waited outside their block for Leila and Kayla's mom. Her boyfriend worked at the used car dealership and had got her a deal on a Volvo, and she could fit five girls on the back seat if everyone half-sat on the lap of the next. We all knew the measures of our thighs exactly, knew them at their best (when we sucked in and stood tall in front of the mirror until we saw a gap) and at their worst (when we sat on the school bus and our skin swamped out like boxed mashed potato when we added the water). All the eighth-grade girls were dressed up. They wore their best denim shorts, every plastic bracelet and bangle they owned on one wrist, t-shirts cut just below their bras or scalloped around the neck so the sleeves dropped off their shoulders. Their hair was braided or gelled or straightened, and their lips were all the same brown from removing and reapplying a dozen shades of color. When they smiled, we saw scraps of tissue paper stuck between the bands of their braces, fluttering with their excited breath.

It was a Saturday and we had nothing to do like every other day of our lives. None of our usual routines seemed appealing. Normally, we spent our time making snacks. We were obsessed with the microwave. We warmed up pink milk, put whatever we could find in tortillas and blasted them until they were crisp and melted and delicious. We talked about boys and agreed to never like the same one. We wrote our phone numbers on scraps of paper and left them in cereal boxes at the grocery store. We waited for someone to call us. No one ever did. We played MASH over and over and never got bored, it never got less funny that one of us was going to have to marry our PE teacher, live in a trash bag, and clean gas station bathrooms, even though some of our moms were cleaners so it wasn't that funny.

But that day we were restless. Every time one of us suggested something to do, we shrieked "Boring!" until she hushed. The big girls were gone and we sensed something was being hidden from us. Far away we could see a storm, a creeping shadow interrupting the baby-blue sky. We could see the distant white forks of lightning spiking and shutting down the roller coasters in the distant parks. We loved storm time, loved to push it with our mothers by staying in the pool even when they shouted at us to get out. The rule was that when there were seven seconds between thunder and lightning, we had to move, because storms could move fast and if we were in the water when the lightning hit, well, we didn't know anyone it had happened to, but we could imagine it. We'd be sizzled like the tortillas in the microwave, crisp and dark and smoking. When we talked about our favorite way to die, we always chose this fate, better, we decided, than freezing or drowning or being shot. Leila had once plugged in her fridge and a blue flame had snuck out of the socket. She said she felt the flame go through her whole body. "Like it licked me," she said, and she showed us her arm where the black hair grew in swirls. "These all stood up," she said, and our mouths watered. This was before we started waxing our arms.

"Let's follow the Volvo," said Leila.

We ran as fast as we could, down the apartment stairs, through the red bark chips on the playground, along the hot road between our blocks, squealing as the tarmac stung our bare feet, relieved when we reached the cool grass and sand of the construction site. We could see the Volvo pause ahead of us at the Falls Landing lights. We ducked around the show home, hopped the beams of the construction site, and sprinted the final stretch, the white wall leering over us. It was so tall that it made the beautiful Falls Landing entrance look stupid and miniature, like the rides we disdained in the theme parks with no height restrictions. We crept around the corner to see the Volvo slide through the black-spiked gates. We snuck close to the glass gatehouse. There were two orange trees on either side of it, their fruit perfect and palm sized. A fountain cascaded over the roof of the gatehouse and into two glittering pools at its sides. We knew that fat and gorgeous goldfish swam in the pools but we had never gotten close enough to see them before the gate man chased us away. We loved the gate man even though he hated us. We loved his uniform with the black and gold brocade trim, and we dreamed about living in his little glass house with a mini TV and some pet fish.

The gate man saw us and ran out of his booth, clapping his hands at us. We growled and hissed and yowled back, playing our part. One of us darted forward, but when he got close, another of us would tap him on the shoulder and run when he whirled around. We shook our bangled wrists and swore like Isabel's mamaie had taught us in Romanian. We didn't know what it meant but later we learned it went something like: your mom made you on sunflower seeds.

We tortured the gate man until he said he would call the cops, and then we fled back to the construction site. We looked in the window of the show home but no one was ever there during the day. There was half of a cherry pie on the counter, shimmering with roaches. Maybe the day before we would have dared someone to stick a finger in and lick it, but that day we felt too old. We kicked at the rotting wood beams, watched the bugs run out, and squashed a few, and then felt bad about it. We were in the mood where nothing was going to make us happy. Every happiness held its own ruin inside it, like a glass we were about to smash.

The construction site had been abandoned for so many years that in our minds it was a finished place. We couldn't imagine anything else being built there. A few rooms were outlined with concrete, hole-pocked tarps flapping uselessly over them, the show home strange and tall in the center. We remembered when the roof flew off in hurricane season. We'd watched it happen from Christian's window, as our mothers partied by candlelight in the living room. We laughed when we saw chunks of the roof lift off and bounce over toward the highway, until there was a hole we could easily see through from our bedroom windows, right to the grassy ground. There was a billboard next to the show home, as tall as the white wall, showing the original vision for the site: a row of identical brown town houses, the same squares of grass by the front doors, a blond couple blown up into giants in the foreground, clutching a large golden key. We couldn't tell if they were happy or sad about their future, because their features had been drawn on by so many kids, adding mustaches and unibrows, that their faces were two black holes.

We listened. We could hear the noise of Sammy's party beyond the wall.

We stared at the faces for guidance. They seemed to give Leila an idea. We watched, enchanted, as she started to climb one of the flaking billboard legs. Only two of us could follow her, because the bottom of the billboard was too thin for us all to sit on. We clutched to the ropy wood legs, heads shoved up near each other's asses, and Hazel had to stay on the ground, whining, "What do you see? What do you see?"

Leila stood up, clinging to one side of the board, and, swinging dangerously, one foot balanced, she stretched her neck to look over the wall. "I can see the yard," she said.

The girls were having water balloon fights. The sprinklers were switched on and the air was filled with rainbow shrapnel. The girls crouched together in Sammy's yard, strategizing, hiding behind the thin palms, collecting piles of grenades, and assigning guards. When supplies had dwindled through waves of attack, Leila told us that one girl stuffed two balloons down the front of her bikini top, and soon all the girls were running around with large, wobbling breasts. Then they started body-slamming each other to explode them.

There was a clap of thunder. The lightning struck close. We saw it spike the highway and all the car headlights brightened obediently. The air around us felt tight.

Then the girls at the party went quiet.

"What's happening?" we called to Leila. Our voices were scared and she was powerful. She was suddenly no longer a part of us, and we knew she held her secret a second longer because she could. When she did speak, her voice was lowered to a whisper.

"I don't know," she said. "They're all looking up at something."

She stood on her tiptoes. Her eyes widened, her face glowed.

"It's Sammy," she said. "She's cut off all her hair. Like, all of it."

No one said anything. We did not know what to say. Isabel stood up on the other side of the billboard to look, wobbled, then immediately sat down again.

"She's on the balcony with some blond girl," Isabel said.

"Who?"

"How short?"

"Shorter than short," said Leila. "It's all gone."

Then the rain began and we were afraid we'd fall off the billboard, and now we had something to live for, something to talk about. We were no longer bored. We slid down the billboard posts, cutting our palms on the rungs and the nails, and we ran screaming like we always did in the rain. When we got beneath the shelter of the first block, we shook ourselves free of the water like dogs. We raced up the stairs and lay on the hard concrete that split Christian's and Britney's apartments on the top floor. We dried ourselves and we thought.

No girl we knew had short hair. No one even had a bob. In summer, we all had the same hair, as long as we could coax it, half dead and raggedy by August from a combination of Sun-In, pulling, and chlorine. We thought of our hair like our magic trick. At night, when we met up on the playground after dinner, we let our hair down like a show, sprung it out of our ponytails and buns, let our braids fall over our eyes like a beaded curtain we could coyly peek through. We hid our faces because we were certain that someday someone else would reveal them back to us, tuck our hair behind our ears, and tell us how beautiful we were, had been all along, in secret. None of us could believe Sammy had hacked off her curtain, revealed herself by choice.

We were smart girls. We read the Bible and fairy tales and watched the news, and our mothers had raised us not to be stupid. We knew nothing in this world came easy. We knew love took practice and we vowed to put in the hours. We knew metamorphosis took danger and, most likely, pain.

We started to use the Internet more. We took photos of Leila with her hair tied back and a hoodie up so she looked like a beautiful boy. We made her a blog where we wrote poems about rain and the color gray, and girls from all over America fell in love with her within a week. Then we took photos of Leila pretending to make out with Isabel. They didn't really kiss, they just sucked each other's thumbs. We wanted to break some soft girl hearts. Leila posted the photos and wrote, "Stop telling me how much you love me! I'm taken!" Then she deleted the blog. "They probably think you're dead!" We laughed, and then we pretended to cry like girls who weren't like us, because they were alone and we didn't love them.

We were scared of being alone. Sometimes we'd pick one of us and play a game. We taunted her, showed her how easily she could be left behind. We'd forget to invite her to the grocery store or to the mall or to the pool, and then we'd talk about it after, look at her and say, "Oops!" If she cried, we left her. If she said, "Fuck you!" we let her stay. And the crying ones we allowed back in after a while, too, because they were desperate and we could make them do anything. We'd make her steal nail polish, or we'd make her run across the highway to the median, or we'd get her to tell her mother she was a bitch. Then we'd all make up and stroke each other's hair and tell each other we loved each other and that we would be friends forever. We stuck our thumbs with needles and held the bubble of blood to the light before we played thumb wars. We weren't always mean. We weren't always nice. We worked hard to surprise ourselves.

It was hard to love Sammy because we only saw her at school, always with the blond girl. We watched them together at lunch time, caught glimpses of them in the hallways, their arms loosely linked. We crept close behind them as they ascended the school bus, before they disappeared to the back row, where we were not welcome. We risked some glances from time to time, saw their legs intertwined on the back seat like they were lying down across it. We copied and lay down, too. We looked at the shapes in the dirty roof and pretended we could see the future in them. Sometimes we were kind, maybe if Sammy smiled at us. We painted gorgeous futures for ourselves. Other times, ignored for days, we picked the weakest of us and said we saw her mother dying tomorrow. We were joking but then Leila's mother almost did die, she had cancer, so we felt bad and only hurt the fathers after that. No one cared about them, we could practically have them drop dead without anyone crying, even after what happened with Britney's dad.

Sometimes we almost forgot about Sammy. Isabel, the last one of us with a dad, learned that her parents were getting divorced. We hated the whole process. They held hands when they told her, there was no fighting, just a love gone listless, and they still all got together at Thanksgiving without a voice raised. It was only Isabel who screamed appropriately and tipped over the sweet potatoes. We refused to be cordial. We would not be born out of sweetness, we were born out of rage, we felt it in our bones. Then Hazel and Jody's dog died. We all loved the dog. He was the size of a chihuahua but had the face of a wolf. Jody had found him stuffed in the trash chute, yapping to hell with his claws clamped to the door. We all wept at the funeral. We all said a few words. We collaged a coffin out of a shoebox, decorated it with snapshots, hearts, infinity signs, and when the time came, Jody let Hazel throw it into the cool dark of the lake. All our mothers teared up at our grace. The truth was, we were pretending, and later we stole Britney's mom's vodka, mixed it with orange juice, and Jody told us the true story as we sipped. She said how the dog's kidneys had given out so he couldn't stop shitting. Hazel sniffled, but we ignored her. Jody had demanded to be at the vet when the death shot was delivered. We were excited by this, because the vet said the dog could kick or moan as he passed over, but Jody sipped her vodka straight from the bottle and told us how the dog went limp, then let out a spiraling fart that made the vet smirk and the student nurse leave the room. It was disgusting to us, that a good dog should exhibit such an undignified death, and we tipped our plastic cups to each other and winced as the vodka whistled down our throats. We felt we understood things more, but we did not want to. Drinking helped. It loosened our laughs, toughened us, made us wild again. We were relieved by this trick and stole more liquor from our mothers. They noticed and hid the bottles, but we always found them again.

They tried to distract us with cheap hobbies, tempting us to make burnt brownies, copy their makeup tutorials, and paint their nails. But it was only when Britney's mom got dumped by a committed bird watcher, leaving behind his weekend bag of tools as he snuck out of the house in a hurry, that we showed any interest in their suggestions.

"Take it," said Britney's mom. "Burn it. Just quit taking my tequila."

We took the boyfriend's bag down to the dock. We removed his books, his whistles, his camouflage shirts. The smell in the bag was sweaty and ancient. We took out a variety of curious tools. We sat around our pile in a cross-legged circle. Leila picked up a pair of binoculars and pointed them immediately toward Falls Landing. We took turns. We turned the lenses until all we could see was the blurry whiteness of the wall, a grainy bright screen, like we'd entered a cheap movie set of heaven.

After the birthday party, we hunted for the blond girl. We didn't have to hunt long. She was suddenly everywhere.

We saw her and her mom on every bench and billboard in town, their hair and teeth the color of peroxide, her mom's candy-pink lips blowing a speech bubble: HAVE YOU GOT WHAT IT TAKES TO BE A STAR? CALL STAR SEARCH TODAY!

"Who's that?" we asked our mothers.

"Mrs. Halliday? She just took over the dance school."

"No! The girl."

"Oh, her daughter. I don't remember, honey. Mia, I think? Yeah. Mia Halliday."

"Mia Halliday," we said.

"Pretty name," said our mothers.

We shrugged.

"It's okay," we said.

We only got to go to Star Search on Tuesdays when Britney's mom taught a dance class. Other days the classes were more expensive. If you paid to do six months of classes with Mia's mother, you got to do an audition at the mall for a casting agent and Stone. Stone ran all the Star Search schools in Florida. He used to be a photographer and he took the headshots everyone wanted, where girls didn't smile and looked so over it all. Sometimes he came by to watch the dance classes, and we noticed how our mothers, watching us, tightened up as soon as he slid in the door. We hardly ever heard him speak. He watched. Very rarely, we heard him shout at our mothers, and though it was rare, we remembered each raised word. Late payments, a door left unlocked, a dirty streak on the mirror. We copied his style when we fought with our mothers, and it always made them cry. We wished they would fight back and beat us, but when we acted like men we always won.

Mia and Sammy recruited girls for the Star Search class. We watched them carefully. We desperately wanted to be picked. We tracked them around the mall and the grocery store and at the movies. We counted how many Star Search business cards they had in their back pockets, checking there were enough for all of us, though secretly we believed only one of us had what it took. We all believed we were the one. We knew this would be the end of us, and we did not care. We wanted to be loved but this was not enough. We wanted to be loved the most. We hovered close by Sammy, by Mia. We wore brighter and brighter outfits. Sometimes we pretended to bump into them to get them to at least look at us, but their eyes flitted past us and away, even when we yelled, "Oh my god, sorry!" right into their ears. We dreamed of their colorful nails winding through our hair, telling us what we suspected the world wanted to say but for some reason could not articulate.

"You're, like, really pretty."

"No one's ever told you that?"

"No way."

"You should model."

"You should be on TV."

We watched who they picked and wondered what it was those girls had that we did not. We blamed our noses, our hips, our cheeks, our teeth, our hair.

We practiced ways to enchant the girls. There was nothing we would not sacrifice for their attention. We studied their nail polish, trying to detect a pattern. Lilac to hot pink to turquoise lasted for weeks, and then burgundy was abandoned for baby blue within a day. We spent a lot of time at the pharmacy, matching shades to names. Pinky Promise, Sugar Fix, Birthday Suit, Malibu Peach, Electra-Cute. What were they trying to say to the world, but especially to us? We plucked the polish from the shelves and painted our nails in the fluorescent bathroom before replacing the bottles. We spread our hands against our legs and admired them all day long. We tried so hard. We quietly copied. It was our first time being quiet doing anything and we were ashamed, but we could not help it. We wanted to be like them, to become ever louder and brighter, but we could feel their futures slipping through our fingers, because we were not stupid. We could tell who was going to peak early and we were not. Even when we were happy, even when we reassured each other we were really living, there was a feeling lying in us that we were not. We squashed our faces against the glass of our own lives. Is this it? we asked. Are we having fun like they have fun? Are we in love like they are in love? We filled up our days following them, watching them, waiting to be invited in. We ran from the truth that the answer was in the question. We were not, and never would be, satisfied.

At the search party, we look for Mia but we cannot find her. This worries us. Leila sends Isabel and Britney to check the wild place, the playground, the pool.

We can see Mia's mom talking to Stone. They sit on a bench with her face on it and the number for Star Search, near the Falls Landing gate. The way she is sitting, she perfectly fits the outline of her picture.

We send Jody to listen behind their heads. Hazel tries to follow her but Jody pushes her back.

"Should we go ahead today?" says Mia's mom.

Stone narrows his eyes. He looks toward the lake and says nothing.

"That father's a drama queen!" Mia's mom says, and a few of the church women, handing out t-shirts, turn to stare at her. Jody is close enough to the bench to touch it when Stone turns around and looks at her.

"Go search for the little angel!" says Mia's mother, shooing Jody away with her long pink nails.

We can see Jody wants to fight or stick out her tongue, because we do not like to be told what to do. But she cannot because we all want Mia's mother and Stone to tell us we are beautiful and make us famous. So Jody smiles, but this is a bad idea because Jody likes candy that stains her teeth blue. She eats it all day long and now her teeth are always a little blue even when she brushes.

"They don't even take them to the dentist anymore," says Mia's mother, rolling her eyes.

Stone doesn't say anything. He still looks at Jody. We all feel it but we do not know what it means. It is a strong look. It burrows through our eyeballs, shines a searching light through the gaps in our bones. Jody runs back to us.

"Creepazoid," she says. We laugh and shiver. We shake our butts a little so we can feel the pepper spray in our pockets. Our moms got us pepper spray from Outdoor World when we were in fifth grade. The canisters are bubblegum pink, and once we tried a squirt in the bathroom and our eyes watered for a week.

Isabel and Britney run over, their faces shiny, their breath quick.

"We've found Mia. She's with Eddie!" whispers Isabel.

"Where?" says Leila.

Isabel looks away toward the lake.

"Where?" says Jody.

Isabel breathes out.

"Where?" says Christian.

"Basketball court," says Britney.

We shake our heads. None of us like to go near the

basketball court. It is the older boys' territory, and we only tried to fight for it once. We do not like to think about lost fights. It was last summer. We were bored and it made us crazy. We crept around the apartments and saw the boys on the court. They were playing skins versus shirts. Britney said, "You know what would be funny?" We agreed immediately. It would be hilarious. We did not think. We ambushed the boys under the dusky floodlights, our cries the cries of ancient battles, pulling off our shirts and chasing the boy with the ball. For a second, we were mesmerizing, we were so bright and bare. We were victorious. Incandescent. Shirtless. Then the second turned into another. The boy with the ball threw it at us immediately, as though he was scared we would touch him to take it. We all froze, realizing our mistake. Our mouths were open in the shape of a laugh that would not come. We felt biblical and stupid. Eddie was the one who collected and returned our shirts, while the boys averted their eyes from us. We flushed, looking at the boys, so long and shameless. Our bodies were almost blinding, we could never ignore them again.

"We'll go," says Leila. "I'm not scared."

Britney digs her flip-flop in the dirt. She picks up an abandoned wine bottle and throws it through the show home window to break the silence. Leila looks at her, and we giggle.

"Come on," says Leila, and we run toward the

apartments. The church women have arrived to look there, too, and we see two of them carrying Eddie's ladder over toward the Falls Landing gate. We try not to stare. One woman is talking to Leila's grandmother through her porch screen. The church woman stands in the grass. The screen casts little dots of light all over Leila's grand-mother's face. The church woman talks loud and slow, like Leila's grandmother is stupid. "Did you see her?" she says. "Where is she? Did you see a man? Or a boy?" We look for a fire ant nest. There is one a few inches from the woman's feet. Jody sticks one of her jeweled flip-flops in the belly of it, and when the rhinestones are covered with ant bod-ies, she tucks it by the raised arch of the church woman's sandaled feet.

"Hi, Nana!" calls Leila, so no one is looking down. Then we run.

We are at the court by the time we hear her scream.

We don't all go up to the basketball court together. We approach like soldiers. Most of us climb up the banyan that stretches over the court, high enough that we are hidden in the leaves, or tucked in the larger branches that form bathtubs we can lie in to listen. The rest of us crouch in a row behind the bougainvillea bushes. We pick a few lan-terns and tip them upside down to see the bugs run out. We give our mothers bougainvillea for their birthdays. We like when they sniff the flowers and tiny bugs run up their nostrils. They scream like little girls and we like to make them scream so we can scream together and feel the same.

Leila, above us in the tree, whistles her bird whistle. We focus, we take it in turns to raise our heads up one by one from behind the bushes.

Eddie stands in the center of the court with some other girls who get off the bus far before us. Mia lies on a metal-ringed bench on the side of the court. She is very still.

The girls stand in a row in front of Eddie. The sun blazes overhead and there is no shade on the court. The girls squint and sweat and look everywhere except at Eddie. He wears his usual basketball shorts, the waistband pulled low to reveal bright boxers. He is shirtless. Eddie's torso is a miracle to us, and we do not even believe in miracles. It looks like it has been cast in gold, soft gold, like Play-Doh. His nipples are two perfect stickers. We want to peel them off him and stick them on our school planners, dot the *i*'s in our names with them on the front of our diaries.

"She didn't say anything to you?" he says. "Nothing?"

The girls shake their heads. One blows a pop of pink gum.

"How many times are you gonna ask us?"

"You know, she's not the first girl to run away."

"Remember Miss Davies's daughter?"

"What happened to her?"

"My mom wouldn't tell me."

"She was just a little kid."

"She didn't run away."

"She wasn't that little."

"My mom said it was her dad who came back for her—"

"They couldn't find him, either, though."

"They never found her?"

"You just moved to this town, didn't you?"

"It's not like they can search the whole lake—"

"Shut up!"

We know Mia's voice. She is the only girl we know who when she screams her voice gets lower. We often hear her scream at her mother outside Star Search, at Sammy when we spy on them at lunch. She does not move at all on the bench. We swear we can see the scream hovering above her face, fuzzing the air, like the mushroom cloud off the nuclear bomb our teacher showed us in social studies. They only showed us the bomb but we used the Internet to see what the bomb did.

The girls shut up.

"She didn't seem weird at all this summer?" Eddie says. "I'm worried about her."

The girls look at each other. The girl with the gum blows another bubble, then lets it hang out the side of her lips. She flicks her head toward Mia.

"Why don't you ask her twenty questions?" She looks at Mia. "Aren't you her best friend? Even after she just stole your boy—"

We all release tiny gasps, but no one notices because

Mia is moving. She stands, jumping up like our mothers sometimes do when they are drunk and suddenly want to hug us. She walks toward the gum girl quickly, the walk they are taught in modeling classes by her mother, one foot in front of the other, and then a foot and hip to the side before the turn. Mia does it beautifully. She stops in front of the girl and juts out a sharp hip.

"You wanna finish that sentence?"

The girl tries to suck in her limp gum but it is stuck in the faint fur below her lip and does not move.

"Say what you wanna say," Mia says. "Go on."

The girl tugs on the gum with her teeth.

"If you've got something to say, say it to my face," Mia says.

She lifts up her index fingernail, which is longer than the others and, we notice, its own shade, just a little darker than the rest. Burgundy Ballroom, we think. Or Outback Aphrodisiac. Mia touches the nail lightly to the girl's cheek, then hooks it under the stuck gum and prizes it off. She sticks out her own tongue and places the gum on its tip. We watch the gum lump travel down her long throat as she swallows it whole.

"Come on," says Eddie. He laughs too loudly. "We were just little kids."

Now that they are on the cusp of high school, we note the difference, the new divides that have been drawn, the before and after of their lives. They were little kids only two months before when they were in middle school, but now they are abandoning us again to high school, while we start eighth grade, and Hazel starts seventh. We are behind, as invisible to them as air now, little kids with large backpacks, our longing eyes as insignificant on their backs as shadows. Soon, they will have cars, and they will disappear from us almost as completely as if we had fed them to the lake.

"Little kids still have hearts, you know," says Mia.

Eddie folds his arms, as though suddenly conscious of his nipples.

"They're no help," says Mia, waving her nails at the girls, who seem to slump in relief.

She takes a packet of cigarettes from the back pocket of her jeans. She shakes one out and looks at it. Then she looks up toward the nearest branch of banyan, the one where Hazel fits because she is the smallest.

"Can we go then?" says one of the girls.

"We should ask her little fan club if anyone saw anything," says Mia. She takes a pink lighter and lights the cigarette. She inhales once so the end burns.

"Who?"

"They're always watching," says Mia. "Haven't you noticed?"

She throws the cigarette like a dart toward the branch, the orange point leading. We hear a shuffle, but Hazel does not scream. The cigarette lands on the concrete and continues to burn quietly.

"You're freaking us out," says one of the girls. She has a long braid that she can't seem to stop picking at.

"We just wanna go home," says another. "Sammy hasn't even talked to us since, like, seventh grade."

"Our moms are gonna kill us."

"They told us not to leave the neighborhood."

"They think I'm at your house!"

"Shit, my mom's gonna see yours at the audition!"

"Shit!"

They giggle.

Mia wriggles her sunglasses. "They're still having the audition today?" she says. "Are you kidding me?" She looks at Eddie, who shrugs.

The girl with the gum smiles. "Sure," she says. "Didn't your mom tell you? Or Stone?"

Mia rolls her eyes. She holds up the pink lighter and flicks it absently.

"Get out of here if you want to go," she says. "No one's stopping you."

The girls stop laughing.

"Go already!" Mia shouts. A few birds rise up from the trees and we shiver. The girls run off the court, struggling to shove open the rusted wire gate. Mia laughs. They finally get the gate open and scatter toward the highway and the search party, the air wet with their retreating whines.

"Why does she always have to be so mean?"

"She's literally crazy!"

Mia moves over to Eddie. She lifts the long nail again. We suddenly all want one. Britney's dad used to keep his thumbnail extra long to pick his teeth, but now we see one long nail can be beautiful. Before she can touch Eddie's skin, so soft looking we swear her nail will cut through it like a knife through a birthday cake, he moves his head away from her.

"Don't," he says. He pulls up his shorts.

Mia smiles. Her smile is the scariest thing about her. We remember that when she first arrived with her mom, her mouth was so crowded with teeth it looked like she had two sets growing at once. She had four snaggleteeth, a crossed quartet at the front. We waited for the day she would get braces and be ruined, become like the rest of us. But the rumor was she'd refused braces so intently that she had even bitten Dr. Grossman's hand when he tried to force in the mold. Her mother was so frustrated she wasn't getting callbacks for photo shoots that it was said she took her to Mexico to fit her for a full set of veneers. Her teeth were perfect when they got back, if slightly too large.

They leave. It is only when they pass the dock that we dare to uncurl ourselves from behind the bougainvillea bushes, drop down from the banyan like the iguanas in winter when it gets too cold and they freeze. We do not say anything to each other. We cannot admit we are scared, so there is nothing to say. We creep back to the search party and hide among our mothers. We wonder what Mia knows. We feel she wants something from us, a secret, and that she will not be afraid to reach right inside of us to wrench it free.

4

ddie and Mia were the first couple we ever knew, unless you count our parents, which we do not. It was rumored that Mia was the one to ask him out, plucking him out of the cafeteria wilderness with a scrunched note: "do you like me?" Two lopsided boxes, marked *yes* and *no*. He must have checked *yes*, which we can imagine because Eddie likes everybody and everybody likes Eddie. Some of us even love him. We love him because he is beautiful and we believe in some ways that he belongs to us.

He lives in a top-floor apartment in A block, with his mom, grandma, Andreas, and Christian. They moved from Venezuela before Eddie was born. We never see their grandma leave the apartment except on New Year's Eve when they all march down the three flights of stairs, dragging suitcases. They sit on the curb with the rest of us to watch the theme park fireworks across the lake. Then they take the bags back upstairs. Christian says it is meant to ensure escape and travel for the new year. We have never seen them go anywhere but we do not say this, we understand because being gone is our only wish, we could not say where to, only that we will be happier there than here.

Andreas is a few years older than Eddie and looks just like him, lean and tan and white-toothed, with the kind of frothy hair we dream of lowering our faces into, like whipped cream on top of a pie. By the time he was thirteen, he was bringing girls back to their shared bedroom in the creases of summer afternoons, the door obediently propped open with textbooks. Their living room was always full of our mothers, drinking coffee until they could drink wine, and they took turns to enter the bedroom every ten minutes or so, the frequency depending on whether the girl wore a cross and whether they knew her mother. It meant that Eddie and Christian were left with nowhere to go, with a kitchen full of mothers and a bedroom full of love, and so we opened our doors and let them spread on our couches, taking careful turns on where we sat, measuring the distance between all our legs and how many times we touched knees. They obediently watched the shows we liked, where women played out versions of our lives with more drug use and pregnancy, slammed doors and tongue piercings, where the couple we rooted for always took the longest, most excruciating time to kiss. Eddie always stayed a boy but Christian became a girl and now he is one of us.

And then Mia stole Eddie away from us. She wrote him the note and took him. After that, he never looked at us anymore.

We watched them eating lunch together, Mia and Eddie and Sammy. It was only ever the three of them, they did not seem to need anyone else. In the chaos of the cafeteria, they stayed still and separate, like film stars sitting among a thousand extras. They took small bites and spoke in whispers. We took notes on where they sat at their table as we blotted the grease from our pizza slices. Outside of school, it was difficult for us to see them in real life. They went to the Falls Landing pool to swim and stopped using ours. They took classes at Star Search on the days we were not allowed in the lot. We watched Eddie's nightly video blog for glimpses. We dissected it religiously. He uploaded photos from throughout the day, then filmed himself in his bedroom late at night. The light of the family laptop threw a radioactive glow over his gorgeous face. He talked for a little while, telling stories we listened to with such intensity that we found it hard to remember afterward what he had said. The best part was when, eyes glazed, he leaned back on his pillow to deliver his signature line into the camera, "Good night, sleepyheads." We left the link live, closing our eyes and listening to the hum of our mothers' computers, sometimes even putting our lips to the hot screens, like he could be contained there in the static, the carefully placed pixels. We hated Mia for taking him away. And we loved Sammy because she had not been chosen. So we chose her.

And then Sammy appeared on the wall, alone.

It was the first day of summer. We were sitting on the dock, cross-legged, making a wall of our bodies so one of us could focus the binoculars on the construction site, where Eddie and his friends were smoking weed. The light draped us in our best shades, pastel orange, pink, soft blue. Even the lake shimmered, and seemed to stink less than usual, with just a hint of dumped fertilizer. We felt we could feel every breath of the boys in our lungs, and we sucked in the air like we were starved for it.

"Sammy's on the wall," said Christian. We all forgot to pretend we weren't watching and whipped our heads around.

Sammy sat on top of the wall, her legs dangling over the edge. She wore a matching pajama set, pink and yellow, with a heart patch on the left side of her chest. We watched Eddie's boys rubbing their heads and yelling. We each took a turn with the binoculars, zoomed in to see Sammy's bare face, her braces, as she leaned back her head and released ball after ball of spit. We could trace the arc of the spit, how white and waxy it was. Every time another one hit a target, she laughed, covering her mouth. The other boys ran, but Eddie stayed.

He stood still. He stared at her like we did and she stopped spitting. And the next night, they were both back, looking at each other in the same still way. For a few days, they seemed to look at each other more than they talked, but every night they were there again, waiting, and soon they grew louder. He shouted up to her, he gestured wildly in a way we never saw him move at school, on his blog, in the slow, languorous poses he adopted with Mia. He paced and shouted and clutched his heart. He jumped up the wall toward Sammy's sneaker as though he thought he could reach her through sheer will. She talked, too, silent

Sammy, her mouth moving fast. She wriggled with excitement and sometimes threw her head back to the sky like she was about to howl. All the cool quietness we so coveted was gone, but they were as mysterious as ever in this mania, this passion, this unashamed care.

We were shocked.

When we spoke about them, we whispered.

We looked at photos of the three of them on Eddie's blog, along with everyone else at school. Then we watched the two of them at night. We looked for signs. Our hearts divided. We were moral girls and we did not believe in infidelity. We thought Eddie was beautiful, simple, and good, like a flower. We never expected his heart to beat in time with our own affections.

Two weeks before Sammy went missing, Eddie went to Britney's apartment. Britney sat frozen on the couch, listening as he asked her mom if he could borrow her boyfriend's ladder, locked up in the bed of his truck below. Britney's mom said she wasn't sure, but Britney stood up, rustled around in the boyfriend's jacket, pulled the key from the ring, and, not able to look at Eddie, pressed it into his hand.

"Britney!" said her mom, but Eddie was already gone.

We huddled together on the dock that night. We had brought snacks but we were too nervous to eat them. We watched Eddie struggle across the construction site, the ladder precarious on his shoulder. Our hearts hummed together. We felt that we were Eddie, we could sense every lean muscle, every taut nerve ending. We knew it was the first time he'd ever questioned how beautiful he was, or if this beauty was enough, and we questioned it, too, felt the logic of the world hover as though deciding where to fall. The sun shifted over the moon and flooded the construction site with romantic light. When Sammy appeared, pulling herself over the wall as gracefully as a girl rising out of a pool in a movie, she saw the ladder and, before we even had time to let go of our breath, confirmed all we had ever suspected of love. She flung herself down the ladder and collapsed into Eddie's arms. They fell all over each other like two tongues trying to tie up a cherry stem.

We lowered the binoculars. We flickered our eyes around. We felt embarrassed. We did not know what to say.

After that night, we did not meet again on the dock. We wanted to keep our admiration hidden, our love safe and unexposed. We gathered in one of our bedrooms to watch, and we made sure the door was locked. We took turns with the binoculars. We watched from the minute Sammy flew down the ladder, how she and Eddie held hands and scuttled into the show home. We watched their shadowy routine. Our binoculars glinted as the sky darkened, the lenses catching the security lights as our mothers moved between one another's apartments. We imagined the Morse code of light in our single window. We wondered if Sammy and Eddie ever saw it, if they wondered what it meant, a message we did not understand but could not stop sending, like a love letter no one would get.

5

When we get back to the construction site, the sun is high and the beer has run out. Kids drop ice cubes down one another's backs. The church women are covered in dirt from their efforts, and the dirt mixes up with sweat, sticky on their skin. We feel itchy with nerves. Leila screams because she finds a caterpillar crawling up her neck, a white caterpillar with red feet. It bites her and all her hairs stand on end. She is mad at us because she thinks one of us put it there, and Britney probably did. She sits on the top step of the show home with a cigarette and does not offer to share.

Britney pretends not to notice and starts playing a band we love on her phone. She dances around in a circle by herself. We can't get too close to her because she likes to hit people in her orbit, and she keeps her hands in fists.

We stay just beyond her reach and play our favorite game, where we compete over what we would do for the love of someone in the band. We have our favorites but we would take any of them. We are honest that way.

"I'd let him bite my thumb off," says Hazel.

"I'd let him run me over with a garbage truck," says Christian.

"Set me on fire and bury me," says Britney.

Leila hears us.

"Garbage truck!" she yells. Leila always decides the

winner. We creep up and curl around her feet. Christian sits between her legs and she strokes his hair.

"Let's play the girls," she says. We all have our favorite character, Mia or Sammy. Leila does the best Mia. Christian does the best Sammy.

"This town is dead as roadkill," he says.

"We're gonna nail the audition," says Leila.

"I can't wait to get to L.A.," says Christian.

Leila raises her phone and we squeeze in, cocking our heads and pursing our lips, shifting our hips to one side. We are careful to not meet the camera's exact eye so we do not see the reality of our faces. Our eyes search the rest of the frame instead. We see the tall white wall rising behind us, and then we shiver, because, like a ghost, we see a shadow standing on the cusp of the wall, hands outstretched like Jesus, head thrown toward the sky. We shout, and our mothers come running, but before anyone can get close to us, we raise our arms and fingers and point to the long line of shadow caused by a girl standing on the wall.

It is Mia.

Every woman, child, and dog turns their head toward her.

Seconds pass.

We wait for the thud.

But she does not fall.

We shift, awkward and unsure. What is she going to do if not jump?

A woman yells, "Don't do it, honey!"

Then another, more angry: "Get your ass down from there!"

An embarrassed silence falls.

Mia's mother comes running, her sunglasses pushed up into her hair. She stands at the base of the wall, hitting it with her fists.

Some of us raise our phones, but our mothers catch us and bat them from our hands.

"How the hell did she get up there?"

"Get that girl down!"

"Call 911!"

"Call the fire department!"

Another silence falls. Even her mother freezes, staring up. There seems to be a telepathic consensus that if we stay still, then so will she. Some of our mothers place their hands over our eyes, so we see the whole thing through woven fingers.

The wall is tall but it is not a skyscraper.

"She probably won't die," Britney whispers.

"Maybe she'll break her spine," says Christian. His mom is doing night school to become a nurse.

"Would she have to wear a brace?" asks Hazel. Hazel has scoliosis and has to wear a brace at night.

"Shut up," says Jody, and we snap quiet.

We wait. We imagine the crunch of bone, the spine

folding in on itself, the cartoon thump, the long silence. The church women edge closer to our mothers. We take tentative steps toward the wall.

Sirens swim slowly through the thick air.

Mia seems to hear them.

She rises onto her tiptoes, and we wince in preparation, the scene stretching wide.

We love her for being there even though no one has brought her a ladder. We wish we could bring her a ladder but we are too late.

She jumps up into the air.

We scream.

She does not fall forward, toward the ground, but backward, out of sight.

In the echoing silence, we hear the comic bounce of a trampoline.

Another woman screams, way too late.

The fire engine trundles uselessly past us, coming to a halt beneath Mia's vacated spot. Two men come out in chunky yellow suits. They stare at the wall. After a minute, they knock on it.

The bounces continue. We hear Mia laughing behind the wall.

We listen to the women.

"That's the girl's best friend."

"Best friend! She's dancing on her grave here."

"Hey, come on now, there's no *g-r-a-v-e-s* here—"

"The kids are here—"

"How many beers have you had?"

"I heard the blonde knows something."

"She wants the other girl out of the audition."

"Are they still doing it today?"

"Last I heard."

"Well, it wouldn't be fair on the rest—"

"It's a shame. The preacher's girl had a pretty face."

"But that hair!"

"The blonde's got big thighs."

"Lisa!"

"What? You can't pretend on camera."

"You know there's been a ransom note?"

"Who said that?"

"Was it Judy?"

"Judy doesn't know shit."

"The blonde knows something."

"No one's found anything?"

"A ladder down by the dock."

"And some flip-flop in the apartments but they don't think it's hers."

"They're going door-to-door in there."

"They rounding up folks in Falls, too?"

"Please, what do you think?"

"Is that girl still bouncing?"

"Rude."

"Brat."

"Spoiled."

"Is he going to get more beer?"

"Do you need a ride to the mall?"

"Where is she?"

"Where is she?"

"Where is she?"

"Where is she?"

"Where is she?"

We know where Sammy is, of course. We always know where Sammy is.

HAZEL

can see my face in the plane window. I am watery, a faint impression losing against the massive sky.

I've been ignoring Jody's messages for months. I tried to get the other girls to come with me, to be a barrier, a buffer between us, but they are too wary of their own unhappiness to want to be near my brand of heartbreak. Jody was the only one who said to come. It was not a long conversation. Silence pushed to its limits on both sides. We have never been good at talking about our feelings. We are not those types of sisters, or people. Emotions are competitive for us, like everything else.

My mother and I had a fight before I got on the plane. She left Florida years ago, as soon as we finished high school. She lives in Texas now with a rich man who in his one short life has managed to marry four wives and produce six daughters, remaining friends with all of them. We used to visit her for the holidays, before Jody got married. Both Jody and I found comfort in Texas, I think, in the sheer force of the rich man's wives and daughters and the magnificent examples of their labor. The Christmas tree touched the ceiling and the surfaces were so clean they seemed to shimmer. The house stank of perfume and masked any human scent. The cut flowers were pumped with sugar water so they were preserved perfectly in the moment of their decapitation. The dogs were small and quiet as toys. There was so much decoration, distraction, but we always ended up somewhere, the three of us, clustered around the kitchen island or huddled on the couch. Music played loudly and there were so many people, so many voices saying the appropriate lines, that the three of us did not have to talk. Sometimes I think my sister, my mother, and I are like one body. My distance from them causes me physical pain, but it is terrible to try to cross it with words. Only when we stand together, close and silent, do I feel whole, and also terrified, because eventually one of us is going to have to speak or move and ruin everything.

My mother agrees that the past is dangerous, which is why she does not understand why Jody is still in Florida, or why I am going to visit her there. She does not understand why none of us talk, except for these strained phone calls where none of us can seem to lie to one another enough to keep a conversation going.

"You idolize something that did not exist," she said when I called her at the airport. Planes carved their way through the sky. "You were miserable children and made my life hell. Why are you acting like your childhood was some glorious place to run back to?"

I hung up on her, because there is no point engaging when she begins to ask questions. My mother is an efficient dictator in her middle age. Her questions are rhetorical and responses will result in excommunication.

Still, a message bloomed before I switched my phone to airplane mode.

"Fly safe," she wrote, followed by a tiny emoji of an airplane and a yellow face blowing a red heart like a bubble of gum. I sent a heart back.

If I remind my mother of something she has said to me in the past, her answer is always the same: "I never said that." I used to be amazed at her self-deception, but now I see I am exactly the same. I used to think people only lied to make their lives mean something. Now I think people lie to make their lives meaningless, because it makes them so much easier to live.

"How can you say that to me?" Luke said before I left. He was sitting on my suitcase to make it shut while I tugged at the zipper, my head next to the stringy waistband of his boxers. It was a less dignified position than I would have liked us to assume for this scene, which I would have summarized as leaving the asshole love of my life. I hated how tragedy always turned to comedy in the last act.

"Say what?" I said. "I haven't said anything."

I recognized his wide eyes, the look my mother used to give to Jody and me when we were cruel to her, when we pretended we did not love her to make her cry.

"Why are you looking at me like that?" I snapped.

"You just said that you never loved me," he said. "You say things like they mean nothing and then pretend you didn't even say them."

75

This was true, and also exactly like my mother. I did not want to admit this, so I left.

When I get off the plane, the air is hot and still, like a person standing too close. I gulp it into my lungs, feeling it weigh down my whole body. I am so relieved that I feel tears itching at my eyes, to feel warmth flow through me, to feel myself expand with heat. I can't believe I have spent so long trying to live through winter. Why would anyone choose a life where it's cold? I take the shuttle to the main terminal. Through the windows, lush green bursts out in carefully manicured pockets, dotted along the tangle of highways, the shiny stretches of car showrooms, the terracotta-colored outlet malls. We slip past billboards. There is an anti-abortion one, a white baby and a black baby smiling gummily, a fake X-ray image over their chests revealing two gray hearts. OUR HEARTS ARE BEATING AT SIX WEEKS! the board reads beneath in bright-red writing. The next one encourages visitors to GET UP CLOSE AND PERSONAL WITH THE OCEAN. There is a picture of a blond girl resting her forehead against a dolphin's, her eyes closed in seeming romantic ecstasy. The next one simply reads, YOUR WIFE'S HOT, BETTER GET THE A/C FIXED, with a 1-800 number. I feel the weight of my phone in my pocket. I immediately want to send photos of these to Luke, and I think how ridiculous that is, that I've spent five years of my life valuing everything I see in terms of how much enjoyment he will get out of it, constantly sending him dumb reminders to love me. I close my eyes.

I had always thought love was supposed to make you selfless, but it made me ridiculously vain.

When we started dating, everything I did that had seemed normal, even dirty, became charmed overnight. My sock drawer, my chipped nail polish, my bad singing voice, eating dinner in bed. All these facts about myself that had rattled around inside me unnoticed were suddenly his to witness. To be loved was just to be watched, or in my case, to imagine you are loved is to imagine you are watched all the time. I preened. I strutted. I imagined he was obsessed with me and so I was obsessed with myself.

The stupid thing was I didn't think about him at all, except once, maybe, right at the end, when I rearranged the living room. I was convinced I could remake our life if I moved the couch far enough from where it usually sat. I shoved the couch out from the wall and screamed. There was a white pile caught up in the carpet. I thought they were maggots, but they were so still. I crouched down. When I got closer, I saw they were fingernail clippings, five years' worth of fingernail clippings dropped behind the couch, chewed off and discarded back there without me noticing, forming this impressive mound. I hadn't even realized he bit his nails. It seemed the first true thing I knew about him. I left them there. The couch stayed where it was.

It was all a lie, which was a relief, in a way, but it still makes me feel like vomiting.

He went to visit his younger brother in college, went to some party, and slept with a girl in her senior year of high school, someone's sister. I only found out because the girl messaged me to tell him to please stop messaging her. I looked through her pictures, found the night in question, saw her, a girl in short-shorts, hair as healthy as a horse's tail, a video of her dancing. She danced the way teenagers dance now, barely moving, their wrists, heads, hips juddering in apathetic zigzags.

"Can you make him stop?" she wrote. "It's creeping me out."

Underneath, she wrote, "sorry btw."

I found the apology moving. I said it to myself aloud, like a mantra against the bad thoughts crashing against my brain. Sorry btw. Sorry btw. The *btw*. She could have gotten away with saying nothing, but she remembered my feelings in the end.

He did not say sorry.

"She's psychotic," he said when I showed him the message. First, he denied it. Then, he admitted to the sex but denied the messages. Finally, he said it was her who started it.

"She's eighteen," he said. "It wasn't, like, weird."

I nodded.

"I love you," he said.

"Mh-mhm," I said. I felt like a therapist assuring him I was listening. "Mh-mhm, mh-mhm," I said. Eventually, I liked the sound of the *mh-mhm*s more than what he was saying, that this flimsy love, three thrown-out sounds, was what I had sacrificed my life for. I started mh-mhm'ing louder and louder, until I was screaming at him.

"Are you okay?" he said.

I told him about finding the fingernails.

"You're disgusting," I said.

"That was you," he said. "You bite your nails and then you're too lazy to get up to throw the pieces away. I see you do it all the time."

He held up his hand.

His nails were long and beautifully mooned.

I looked at my own.

The nails were ragged and torn, soft and chewy.

Somehow, this relieved me.

"I never loved you," I said. This was not true, exactly. I loved his body, that soft, familiar sack. How many times had I burrowed into him, wishing only to be smaller, to chisel myself down until, cell-like, I could slip inside him? I did not love the stranger he turned out to be, but I loved the parts of him he had no control over, his bones, the way he moved. I called all the girls, seeking refuge, a quick escape. I sent old pictures of us, our glossy arms around one another, hair ties burrowed into our wrists. They wrote, "Aw." They wrote, "I miss you." I called and they did not answer. They had families, jobs, and lives. I called Jody last, the same meanness in me, or fear, of never picking her first. "You're the only one who ever really loved me, aren't you?" I cried, drunk into my phone, curled on the couch while Luke snored on the bed. She didn't say anything for a long time. I became angrier, wondering why she couldn't be the kind of sister to tell me things were okay, that I was amazing and he was a douchebag, why we couldn't laugh or reassure each other that life and people were ultimately good. But none of the women in my family think this. Finally, she coughed, awkwardly, and invited me to come over. "I have something to show you," she said. "The baby?" I said. She'd had a baby not long before. I tried to sound more excited, like that was why I had called. "The baby!" I cried. "Of course!" "Not the baby," she said. I was relieved. I booked a ticket straightaway.

I walk out of the airport. The heat is thick and uncomfortable, like the air is made of Styrofoam.

Jody is directly outside the doors. When she sees me, she screams, runs out of the car, and throws her arms around me. We are the same height but she tucks her head down like a turtle so it is pressed into my neck. She smells slightly expired, a smell I've noticed on all people with babies.

I go rigid in her arms, and then try to overcompensate by swooping my arms around her too tightly. I did not expect her to hug me. "Hey," she says, pushing me back to arm's length. We hold the pose a second longer until it feels false. I'm relieved when she lets go of me to take my suitcase and strides over to the back of the car.

It has been five years since I have seen her, five years since I have been my actual self, an unloved, alone person. I slide into the SUV and slump into the seat. There is an open can of iced tea in the cupholder, a few brown envelopes, a cell phone. I look back. A baby stares at me, his eyes a deep gold beneath a thick crown of black hair. I realize with a shot of cold horror that I've completely forgotten his name. She did not tell my mother or me that she was pregnant and we've hardly spoken since he was born. I did send her a cheap teddy bear from my mother and me, a clear plastic cover over the chest revealing a light-up heart inside it. I knew she would hate it.

"I'm an auntie!" I say. I reach back toward the baby, but do not know what to do with my hand when it arrives close to him. I pause, then tap him on the knee, and a thought appears whole in my mind, one that is summoned without my control or consent: she is my sister before she is your mother, and she belongs to me. He does not start to cry, even though the tap is more of a knock. I withdraw my hand quickly, embarrassed, and turn around.

"You want to pick something to listen to?" Jody says.

She has put on sunglasses, which is a relief. I don't want to think about how our faces have changed.

"The radio's fine," I say. I lean over and turn it up. She's concentrating on getting out into the mania of the lanes. I wind down my window slightly to feel the trash-infused air blow past my face. At least this is familiar.

Jody has been a great driver since she was thirteen, and our mother used to get her to park the car when we had dinner at the mall food court and she drank too many beers. Jody veers between lanes, one hand on the wheel, the other used for taking slugs of iced tea. I am relieved that she has not asked me about my flight or how I am, and then as the silence continues, I am offended she hasn't.

"How are you?" I say, finally, as we soar past a steak-house, an indoor skating rink, a giant grocery store, a pastel-yellow motel claiming WE'RE CHEAP AND DISCREET. A homeless man sits beneath a traffic light in a camping chair, holding a cardboard sign reading THERE IS NO OCEAN IN OCEAN WORLD.

"Oh, I'm okay," she says. "I'm excited you're here."

I think she is going to tell me how lonely she is, how glad she is to see me, how much she loves me. Perhaps she will share her own tale of heartbreak and woe. Post-partum blues. An impending divorce. Perhaps her husband also fucked a senior in high school. Maybe even a junior. I feel my old beautiful feathers rustle and puff up a little, see myself in the side mirror, ready to pity her. I smile. My greasy hair! The bags under my eyes! The sauce stain on my shirt! Charming, beautiful, loved by at least somebody.

"I've found something in the lake," she says. "I told the girls, too, but none of them would come see it. Can you believe that? Not one of them. They all think I'm crazy. But I've been watching it."

The baby begins to cry.

Even his cry is weirdly beautiful, plaintive as a pop ballad.

She leans over and turns up the radio to drown him out, and then reaches over to grab my hand. I notice her nails are long. They dig into my hand like someone trying to hang on to a cliff.

"I knew you'd understand," she says.

My hand is limp and unenthused, toeing her over the edge.

"I might have to leave tomorrow," I say. "I'm sorry. Work's really crazy, I just came—"

"It's okay, we'll go see it tonight," she says.

I drop her hand. I have ignored her weird messages for a long time, although she has started sending them more frequently over the past year. Long links that take up the whole of my phone screen directing me to incomprehensible forums with names like "The Truth About Bigfoot." Expired video links, blurry photos. I used to send back thumbs-up emojis without looking at them. I remember my mother forwarding me one of these messages, asking me to speak to Jody about it, explaining that she wasn't answering my mother's calls, but I did not. I did what I always did, which was to disappear for a few months, then text "miss you!!!!!" with no explanation. I used exclamation points instead of excuses. Perhaps this is why I haven't made any friends since I was thirteen, and technically, they were my sister's friends anyway.

The baby's cry harmonizes with the disco beat of the song. Jody starts to sing over it, too, making up words and notes.

The whole plane ride I had prepared my spiel about the tragedy of my life. I was sure she'd be fascinated but I have forgotten that she has never been fascinated by me, and that no one is fascinated by someone who is alone.

She looks at me, wriggles her sunglasses, as if daring me to join in her song.

What the hell? I think. I do. I go low when she goes high. I warble when she belts. We always used to sing together. I still can't believe how wonderful I thought we always sounded, doing performances for our mother, until we applied to be on a reality show when we were teenagers and our mother had to tell us that we could not sing. We still sound beautiful to me, so loud and determined. The baby stops crying and listens, eyeing us warily. The city streams past us, the endless palms and suburbs. I stick my hand out of the window and hold the air, squeeze it like a stress ball. I want the drive to last forever, for us to be suspended in this singing, the baby silent, but then we're turning into her house, and her stepdaughter is sitting on the driveway, throwing a tennis ball against the garage door. There is a standoff as Jody honks the horn and turns in, but the girl doesn't move. I'm surprised at how far Jody noses the front of the car, almost against the girl's back, until the girl gets up and throws out both middle fingers, her whole face taut with fury. The girl runs away into the house. The baby starts to cry again.

"He's like a weather vane for feelings," Jody says, getting out of the car and hoisting him out of the back seat like he's a grocery bag. "And I'm always pissed off."

The house is designed in the way of old Florida houses to be as dark as possible. The blinds are down and brown linoleum puffs up under my bare feet. By the door, there is a pile of shoes, and the floor beneath is covered in gray grit, relics from beach days. The furniture is mostly dark wood, chipped, missing knobs or panels, and full of plastic cups, dishes, newspapers, wires, grocery bags. Socks, notebooks, flashcards, receipts, coins are littered along the hallway. I notice a few curled shells of dead roaches in the carpet borders. There is a specifically Floridan smell, the stink of America (microwaved plastic, air freshener, hot oil) mixed with mildew and something else, something ancient, rotting, and sweaty, possibly life. I want to lie down in the hallway and close my eyes. The smell is so familiar it's like I'm rocking back in the womb.

I follow Jody into the kitchen. She immediately fetches two wineglasses, retrieves a half-full bottle of yellowish wine from the side of the fridge, and pours two glasses. The baby seems to accept his fate to be bounced around as long as he is close to her. A laptop is open on the counter, surrounded by what looks like a child's homework. I recognize the careful date in the corner. Jody opens the computer, types, then swings the screen around to face me.

The video is called "Unidentified Florida Object." She presses play.

I watch, pick up my wine.

There is a family, passing around a camcorder and waving, the footage grainy, flashes of sunlight intermittently clouding the shot. They are backing up a boat toward a lake.

The shot is terrible, the camcorder having been handed to the little girl, who is swinging it around and making the landscape swirl. Still, I notice the beige towers, the fertilizer factory, the wide expanse of water, completely still.

"Is that—?" I say, but I feel stupid for asking. It obviously is.

She sips her wine, her eyes wide. She nods. The baby burrows into her shoulder, and I look back at the screen.

The video cuts out, returns. The family is on the boat. The father and the son have fishing poles, the mother is reading, her face hidden in the shadow of a huge sun hat. The little girl swings the camera inside her father's ear, centers a pimple on her brother's chin. She films the clouds, translating them in a lisping voice though they all look the same. "Banana," she says. "Hot dog."

I am bored. I have no patience for little girls anymore.

Her family is obviously bored, too. They do not seem to hear her, even when she starts to talk excitedly, and then fearfully, and then starts to scream.

She lifts a pink finger and turns the camera toward the lake.

The sun shines in such a way that one square of the dark water turns transparent.

A shape grows beneath the water.

Her family sees it, too. There is a sharp reel as the fishing lines are drawn in.

The faintest hump of skin cracks the water.

I am completely still. My breath ripples the wine in my hand.

Then the girl drops the camera. The shot turns upward and fills with sky, catching for a second a pink face, so stretched and strange that it could have belonged to any member of the family. A spray of rainbow droplets lands on the camera lens. A shadow encases the boat, stark under the huge blue sky, a shadow with no discernible source.

The laptop is shut, hard. I look up and see Jody's husband, Luis, his hand still holding the laptop closed.

"Hazel," he says. "It's so good to see you. We've missed you."

He takes the baby from Jody and jiggles him, then picks up one of the baby's small hands and says, "Hi, Auntie Hazel!"

I raise my hand reluctantly.

Jody doesn't say anything. She picks up the bottle and her glass and moves outside to the small patio, sliding the glass door shut behind her.

Luis winces. He looks at me.

"Maybe you can help," he says. "Help her move on from this? She's been getting really obsessed lately. Especially since the baby."

His daughter comes in. She goes to the fridge and starts to make herself a snack plate, a cheese stick, some leftover ziti, a popsicle. She arranges them carefully on her plate. Luis and I watch her in silence.

"I'm fascinating, I know," she says, plucking a fork out of a drawer, widening her eyes at both of us in imitation.

"Healthy choices," says her dad, and the girl rolls her eyes. "We've got dinner, you know."

She looks at me.

"Are you going to get Jody to stop being such a psycho?" she asks.

I shrug.

"I don't know," I say.

"Why are you even here, then?" she says.

"Jennifer," says her dad. "Don't speak to your aunt like that. You haven't even said hello."

"I've met her, like, twice," Jennifer says, unpeeling the cheese stick. "Who even is she?"

I slip out the screen door onto the porch. I feel refreshed by Jennifer's question, then devastated by it, then refreshed again. There are two chairs next to Jody, a camping chair and a rocker. I sit on the rocker. Wicker pokes me in the ass. We are surrounded by dying plants. Through the porch screen, I can see a yard full of rusting toys, a chair frame with no seat, a collapsed clothesline, all leading down to a small, low lake. A screen of insects hums above its surface. A shopping cart sticks out of its center, the wheels spinning slowly with the first curls of storm wind.

"So what do you think of the video?" Jody says. "I swear there's really something in the lake. I see it some nights."

"What happened to that family?" I ask.

"No one knows," she says. "They were tourists. Nothing was ever reported. But no one's seen them again. Some of us think it's a cover-up. Florida government, you know, climate change, chemical runoff. Some of us think it's extraterrestrial, left over from a meteorite or something."

"But who uploaded the video of it?"

"Maybe a defector. Trying to get the truth out."

"Not the family?"

"You think the family survived that?"

"Well, if the family didn't, how would the camera?"

She shakes her head.

"You're not here," she says. "You don't understand."

I take a sip of wine.

She stares straight ahead.

"There's big money in it, I think," she says. "If I can prove something weird is in there. It could be the Loch Ness of Florida, you know?"

I suddenly want to lie my head in her lap. It has been so long that I can't believe I was ever that comfortable with another person, that I could touch another body with no fear or care.

I think of the cool darkness of the lake, the creature in the light beam. The risen shadow.

I decide I would rather be crazy if it means we can at least be crazy together.

"Can we go look, then?" I say.

We are giggly and stupid from the wine.

"Let's sneak out," she says.

We look back through the glass. Jennifer is adding to the pile of homework, Luis is stirring something in a pot on the stove, the baby attached to his chest. The baby is the only one who looks at us, raising a pudgy fist in protest as a pacifier falls from his mouth.

"Quick," Jody says. She bangs open the screen door and we step out onto the sandy grass. She holds my hand and we run along the side of the house. My breath beats in my throat. I can't remember the last time I ran anywhere. We sprint to the car like we are being chased. She has the keys in her jean shorts, and we slide into the car, our thighs instantly adhering to the hot leather. I reach for the seat belt but the silver stings to the touch. We drive off in a dramatic screech, unbound, the headlights two white lines before us. The houses are low and flat, like animals lying in the grass. The air is sticky with the effort of trying to make some rain. We roll down the windows as the first thunder claps and we hit the highway as the first curtain of rain falls. The air is full of creamy dark clouds, struck by veins of lightning. I want to live inside this moment forever, but if I've learned anything, it's that even movement becomes another kind of stillness if you force it to last too long. She seems to know this, too. We pull into a gas station and watch the rest of the storm shimmy its way past us in silence. It rains all through the sunset, and by the time it wraps up, it's dark.

"This is good," she says. "It comes out when it rains."

We buy Twizzlers, Slim Jims, chips, and another two bottles of cheap cold wine. We buy cigarettes and chain-smoke them out of the windows.

My throat starts to hurt by the time we pull up to

the lake. The construction site is a grocery store now. The apartments have been painted white. The new blocks shine proudly in the dark. On the other side of us, Falls Landing is gone, replaced by rows of beige town houses. The gate man and his house are gone, too, but the wall remains, leering out of the dark.

I stare at the lake, trying not to commit anything else to memory. I already know I will not want to remember this night. I drink more wine.

We drive across the empty parking lot, traversing the blue stillness beneath the floodlights. We maneuver over a small curb into the shadows, over a short stretch of grass, right up to the edge of the lake.

The headlights of the car shine across the still water. The lake is so solid that it could be a road. I look at Jody, half expecting her to slam the gas, throw us forward, but she turns off the radio, the engine, the lights.

Suddenly, we're smothered in darkness.

We stare out across the water. I wait for my eyes to adjust but no shapes appear, only distant dots of light across the lake.

"You think I'm crazy," she says.

"You really think there's something living in there?" I say.

We watch. She starts talking quickly, her words incomprehensibly scientific and slurred, something about radar and tests and her new friend Cathy who works at Ocean

World and who spends most nights with her in this spot. I try not to be jealous of Cathy. I reach for her hand and she shuts up the longer I hold it, accepting my pity, though she won't look at me. I imagine she is crying. We continue to watch the water for a few long minutes that pass through awkwardness, cross into a silence that starts to feel impossible, like it will only be broken by a holy sound or word. I have nothing to offer, and think that maybe we will never be able to speak again. Then Jody drops my hand. She reaches for the key, and I turn to her, noting her eyes are bone dry. I face the windshield again, disappointed. She turns the headlights on, and there, as close as our own reflections, I see a creature adhered to the glass. It is achingly familiar, like a part of my own body that has been wrenched out and displayed. I grab her hand again, dig my nails in so hard we are attached. As the scream fills my mouth, I realize what a fool I have been all these years, that it was never Luke, or myself, who I felt watching me, not ever, not once.

The search slows down. Finding the ladder caused a brief flurry of excitement but they have not found anything else, and the ladder has been left abandoned on its side beneath the wall, burning in the sun. A large tent has been put up beside the town house billboard, the walls folded back so we can see in. Some pallets have been pushed together to form a stage and Sammy's dad paces across it, swinging a portable microphone and mumbling, "Where is she?" "Where is she?" "Where is she?" His white suit has dirty legs.

Britney's mom winds a finger by her head.

"Starting to get a little cuckoo round here," she says.

They gather us all together, our little brothers and sisters, too, herding us in.

"Let's get you to the audition," they say.

"A better place for kids," they say, patting our cheeks.

"I was sure they'd have found her by now."

"It's only been what, twelve hours?"

"My girl's been gone for longer than that before."

"And you didn't call out God's army—"

"They would have laughed if I tried."

"Last week, Kayla told me she was going to stay with some friend's uncle at the beach—"

"Bullshit?"

"Uh-huh. She used my credit card to get McDonald's in Tallahassee at four in the morning—"

"What'd she say when she got back?"

"Oh, she told me all about how they went to some fancy seafood restaurant and ate bad crab. Said she was in bed all weekend."

"Bullshit?"

"Total bullshit. Not a flicker in her face. And when I told her I knew, do you know what she did?"

Britney's mom flips a finger.

"No, not even that. She just laughed."

"What a little bitch!"

"Lisa!"

"Sorry."

"I don't trust a word these girls say."

They look at us then. We gaze at them innocently.

"We just hope she's okay," says Leila, sticking out her lip.

"It's kinda scary," says Hazel.

Christian snorts and has to hide his face in Jody's shoulder. Jody's face does not move at all. Isabel and Britney squint at the sun to make their eyes water.

"No place here for our little girls!" our mothers say.

We can't all fit in the cars so we play Rock Paper Scissors, but when Leila loses and has to walk, we all want to walk with her. Britney gets mad and almost goes in the car, but we know she does not like to be alone, so we all walk along the highway to the mall. Our moms are scared we'll get heatstroke but we do not care. We've had heatstroke before. Once Hazel turned purple for a whole day, and another time Christian passed out and said the girls on the Arabian Nights billboard told him he was going to heaven. Along every telephone pole and streetlight Sammy's face stares out at us, and we make a game of it, every time we see another we yell, "Where is she?" as loudly as we can. We laugh until we see a church woman poking around on the other side of the highway, cars streaming between us. She holds her staple gun in the air and yells something at us we cannot hear, but we can tell it is mean.

Kids from all over the state are in cars blocking the highway. The audition starts at two. The slots are three minutes long, and kids can fill the time with a monologue, or a song, or a dance, or if they are models, a slow pace back and forth across the stage, showing they can jerk out both hips and pivot, and they don't quiver even with their baby ankles balanced on skinny heels. In the back windows of the cars, we can see the hanging, pressed outfits, the plain t-shirts without logo or pattern, the stiff blue jeans, the uniform of America that can handle the mall's blazing light and not fuzz up on camera. Some of the windows are fogged up and tacky from last-minute puffs of hairspray and fake tan.

Soon we see the mall ahead like a great white cathedral. We walk along the pocked sidewalk. We try to step on all the cracks but there are so many cracks. No one ever walks anywhere so no one fixes the sidewalks.

Along the road, we sing all the songs from the school musicals. We have never been cast but when we sing together we are all the stars of the show. We leave a stream of sound along the highway that drowns out the slow drone of the cars. We throw out middle fingers and blow kisses and Britney even moons a truck, because the traffic is so thick that we can outrun them in case they find us too irresistible and kidnap us.

We feel chased, it doesn't matter if it's only by our own shadows.

We run beneath the big blue sky toward the mall.

We feel maniacal with hope.

The food court is full by the time we arrive. The regular stage is set up in front of the big fountain, two banners with Mia's mother's face on either side of it, so they seem to be in conversation with each other:

"Do you have what it takes?"

"Do you have what it takes?"

We go and get a Chinese chicken sample on a toothpick, and then we scare some younger girls out of a booth, brandishing our toothpicks when they roll their eyes. Some of us have to sit cross-legged on the table, and the rest of us kneel up on the benches to see. We can see Isabel's and Britney's moms helping Mia's mother, adjusting the heads of microphones. Jody and Hazel's mom crouches over a boom box, pressing buttons wildly and looking stressed.

The food court is full but no one is eating. The girls stand around looking bored at the salad bar, the pizza place, the pretzel stand, the big cookie booth. Mothers are everywhere, talking rapidly, squeezing and rubbing at girls' faces, pulling girls' hair.

"The girl hasn't showed up yet?"

"What girl?"

"The preacher's daughter!"

"Who?"

"You been living on Mars?"

"Oh, I don't care right now. I've been trying to get this girl's hair to stay still for six hours!"

"You got spray?"

"Please, I'm going home to a house of poisoned dogs with how many cans I've emptied this morning."

"Just kidding, sweetheart!"

"Don't cry—the mascara!"

We stare up at the glass roof of the mall. It is so crusted with bird shit that the never-not-blue sky looks gray. We look at the kids waiting to audition. The light makes them look like they are about to throw up. The mothers seem to realize this and they are piling on blush, bronzer, glitter. All the kids look the same. They bare small teeth, their eyes water. We know the tricks. We know when a mom's rubbed Vaseline into a kid's gums, some extra pain in their grin. It is easy to tell when a tooth whitening has gone too far.

We do not like looking at them. We start to fidget.

Their eyelashes are gummy with mascara, their cheekbones are never going to sprout. They remind us of us. We think that maybe we should give up. We could stop watching. We could stop dancing. We see new lives open up before us. We could try harder in algebra, work at the food court, get boyfriends. We could get cars, get our own apartments, eventually push some babies out of our bellies. We could become like our mothers. We think of our mothers when we love them the most, which is always just after we hate them the most. There have been blue days and weeks when they do not come when we call them, as if they are insisting they do not belong to us, even when we tell them there is no cereal in the house. They always come back to us when we do not expect it. They arrive at breakfast or on our balconies. They clutch us to them and say sorry. They talk over our heads. They think their words are riddles to us, but they are not. We understand they are sad because they are waiting to be chosen by one in their carousel of men. They pat our heads when we tell them this, but they do not hear us. "You don't understand anything," they say, and we get so angry we sometimes send them straight back to their beds again.

Then Eddie and Mia arrive and our mothers tumble out of our heads.

The pair poses for a moment in the glass frame of the puffing automatic doors, caught like celebrities on a red carpet.

Eddie wears basketball shorts, a basketball shirt, shiny sneakers. Mia wears a cherry-red t-shirt and a tiny denim skirt. Her hair is pulled into a high-arched ponytail. Her nails clutch Eddie's arm.

"Yucatan If You Want," says Christian.

"Funny Bunny?" says Britney.

"Taupe-less Beach and Aphrodite's Pink Nightie?" says Hazel.

"It's a hundred percent Yucatan," says Isabel.

We look to Leila for confirmation but she says nothing, she does not seem to be listening to us.

We follow Mia and Eddie with our eyes. We feel the ripple they send through the food court. A family of six freezes in front of us as they pass, brandishing bobby pins toward the head of a tiny girl in a tutu. Straws miss lips. Jokes lose their punch lines. Gossip loses its pull. Mia's mother runs over to them. She ignores Eddie and pulls Mia away, prying at Mia's sunglasses. Mia ducks and hits away her mother's hand.

Isabel's mom fusses with the microphone. She moves her mouth but we cannot hear her.

"We can't hear you, mom!" yells Isabel.

Isabel's mom blushes and hits the end of the micro-phone. A screech shoots out through the mall. Everyone shrieks and slaps their ears closed, the auditionees the most theatrically.

Mia's mother runs onto the stage and pushes Isabel's

mom aside. We laugh when Isabel's mom sticks her tongue out at Mia's mother's back.

"Okay, ladies and gentlemen!" cries Mia's mother. "Welcome to the Star Search!"

She looks at Jody and Hazel's mom, who presses a button hopefully. Loud explosions ring out through the speakers. Mia's mom pauses for applause. When none arrives, she starts to clap violently herself. A few others join in from the crowd.

"Let me hear you!" Mia's mother screams. "Have you got what it takes?"

"Yeah!" shouts the little girl in the tutu.

"Aw," says the food court.

A few other kids shout out, prodded by their mothers.

"Yes!"

"Yeah!"

"Yes!"

The food court stays silent.

"Well, today we're gonna find out! It could be your lucky day. We're offering callbacks, and even, I have had it confirmed"—she drops her voice from a scream to a whisper—"a plane ticket straight to Hollywood!"

The crowd rustles with excitement.

She reads out a list of names from a clipboard, pausing after each one to place a hand on her heart and say, "Thank you." She does not thank our mothers. Then she introduces the agent. One little girl in the line starts to cry when Mia's mother says the name of an actor the agent represents. He has curly hair that kills us all, and we guess it is too much for the little girl and her doll-sized heart to handle.

"I'd let him put a Q-tip too far in my ear," whispers Christian.

"I'd let him run over my foot," says Jody.

"I'd let him chew my lips off," says Britney.

"Ew, Britney," says Leila, and she does not even say who won.

We shut up because the agent comes out of the Star Search offices. It has never been a woman before. Stone is behind her. When they pass by, the crowd tightens up like the two of them are cops. Stone leads her toward the two folding chairs in front of the stage and the plastic table waiting for them, designated with a gold plastic cloth. His hand is against the agent's back. When they sit down, his hand stays, we can see between the gap in the folding chair. We watch as she reaches around with her own hand to remove it. He rests the hand between his legs. His knees widen.

The audition begins.

The first girl cries with nerves and walks off early. While her time runs down on the clock, we can all hear her mother screaming at her husband.

"I should never have changed my name to Abbot! My baby's always the first one off the diving board!"

The next girl seems to try to compensate for Abbot by performing her monologue about her mother's chemotherapy with a cheery optimism, baring her teeth to the back of the room.

Then there is a beautiful boy dancer. His body seems elastic. His legs whack the side of his head when he kicks them up, his tight afro skims the floor when he leans back. Everyone claps for him, including the agent, but she doesn't write his name.

After a dozen kids with no names written down, they start to get wilder, louder. They drop to the ground and do the worm, they hold their big notes even when the song is finished.

But the agent does not write down a single name. There is a break when the younger ones finish. Mothers calm down and pretend to be interested in other people's children. The kids pull out painful hairstyles and play tag around the fountain, scooping out the coins dumb tourists throw in the water.

Then the teenagers start. They cry about sexy photos sent around school. They cry about being dumped. They cry about death. They cry about their parents getting divorced. No one mentions abortions, though we know some of the girls have held their mom's hands on the way to Planned Parenthood. No one talks about pills, though we know half the boys have baggies of them rattling in the pockets of their cargo shorts. We are bored, watching their faces fake feeling under the lights. They look gray and sweaty. We wait impatiently for Mia and Eddie to rise up in the line. Mia is wearing the biggest pair of sunglasses we have ever seen. She wears sunglasses all the time, even in February when the sun gets gauzy. Sometimes we dream of wrenching them from her face. We imagine they make a satisfying sound like the Velcro on our sneakers. We have never seen her eyes. In our dreams, they are black as the black holes of the blond couple on the construction site billboard, with no white left in them at all.

She is before Eddie. We clap fiercely when she climbs onto the stage. She wobbles a little when Eddie shakes his arm free from her, as if she is surprised he is not coming with her. We have never seen her alone and we think of her in her bedroom on the nights Sammy meets Eddie on the wall. We wonder if she watched from her window as Sammy leaped away from her into the sky every night.

We are surprised by how loud our hands are. We look around. Only a few other families are clapping, and they are not families we know. Our mothers and the women from the search party keep their arms firmly by their sides. We watch their painted lips forming whispers, quiet enough that we cannot hear, but we sense they say:

"Where is she?"

"Where is she?"

"Where is she?"

Mia's sunglasses dance with the bright mall light. The rest of her face does not even shiver.

"I'm Mia Halliday," she says. The women fall quiet. The silence is sudden and whole and seems more aggressive than the whispers. We can hear the hydraulic shush of the fountain, the plop of pigeon shit on the glass roof, the low drone of heat lamps keeping the pizza slices, the burrito beef, the teriyaki chicken lukewarm and sweaty.

"Hi, Mia," says the agent. "What are you doing for us today?"

Stone leans over to whisper something in her ear. She shuffles to the edge of her seat away from him, until half her butt hangs over the edge.

"I'm a triple threat," says Mia, sticking her hand on her hip and doing her impressive model-at-the-end-of-a-runway pose.

"Can you take your sunglasses off for me?" says the agent.

Our hearts thump. We open our eyes wider and try not to blink.

Mia fingers the arms of her sunglasses. We see her mother on the side of the stage, miming furiously. "Take! Them! Off!" she mouths.

Mia takes them off.

"Oh my god," says Isabel.

The shape of every pair of sunglasses we have seen her wear that summer has left huge white patches in her extremely tanned face. She has not bothered with eye makeup, and her eyelashes are blonde and stubby. Her eyes are as black as we imagined they would be, or almost black, the color of the lake. We thought they would sparkle, but they are still and dark and reveal exactly nothing.

"You might wanna even that tan out for L.A., honey," says the agent.

The food court laughs.

"Jesus, Mary, and Joseph!"

"She looks like you when you passed out by the pool that Fourth of July—"

"Don't remind me."

"Hush, poor girl—"

"She's embarrassed, look—"

"Oh, don't be soft on her!"

We laugh, too, we cannot help it. Then we bite our lips to stop them betraying us. We do not want to laugh at Mia.

The agent gestures to Isabel's mother above the boom box. She is a nice mom and she starts the song quickly, spiraling the volume up to drown out the crowd's laughter. Mia misses the first bars. She stands still until the crowd quiets. Then, suddenly and awkwardly, she comes to life. She tries to lower herself to the ground for a dance move, sliding one leg out to the side, but she still has her sunglasses clutched in one hand. She almost loses her balance, but she straightens up and shimmies instead, then breaks into a robotic version of the hula.

Then she starts to sing.

We want it to stop. She sounds like Jody and Hazel when they insist on performing their duets for us. We look toward the exit. It is the first time in our lives that we think, We wish we had a drink. Around the court, grandmas plug their ears. Babies begin to cry. Mothers flee, clutching the babies to their chests, and some of the grandmothers shuffle toward the exits, calling back as they pull cigarettes from their huge purses.

"Sorry, honey, I've gotta take a break."

We keep our eyes fixed on Mia. Distracted by the noise, she forgets the lyrics. "La la la!" she sings. "La!" The second-to-last *la* is quiet, the last *la* just a breath. Then she is silent. She stands still while the music beats on around her.

We watch her like we would watch someone dying.

When she stops singing, the fleeing crowd pauses and looks back at the stage, squinting. Mia seems to feel the attention return. We inch forward in our seats. She closes her mouth tight, bends over double, clutches her ankle, and twists her face in mock agony. The music continues perkily as she hobbles toward the edge of the stage.

"Is she hurt?"

"Please, she's faking."

"She'll make all the excuses now."

"At least she's stopped singing."

"Isn't that the Halliday girl?"

"I don't know if *she* has what it *takes*."

Isabel's mom turns off the music, turns quickly to the advertising track, the appliance store that sponsors the auditions. "If you didn't buy from us, you paid too much!" the man screams. People relax. The advert is on every commercial break on every local station, the man's shrill yell like a lullaby we have known all our lives.

As Mia edges her way off the stage, we swear we see her smile, but before we can tell, she trips off the stage.

Her fall is spectacular. She seems to fall upward, into a perfectly horizontal line, before she plummets toward the sticky food court floor, landing on her ass, her legs splayed out in front of her like a rag doll. She crumples up and starts to cry, a cry that seems to contort every tan and pale part of her face. The mall erupts with laughter.

She looks up at Eddie, bent above her, laughing so hard he howls. A little spit flies from his lips and over her white sneakers.

The women around us whisper loudly between giggles.

"Stop laughing!"

"You're laughing!"

"I feel bad for her, they still haven't found her friend—"

"Oh, did you hear she's been climbing over that wall for months to meet that boy—"

"Sure, I've seen her sneaking into that show home—"

"I wish they'd burn that place down—"

"The Halliday girl, you mean?"

"No, the preacher's daughter!"

"With the wetsuit?"

"Lordy lord."

"What boy was she meeting?"

"The one next in line!"

"Well, he is pretty."

"She'll turn up crying at a Greyhound station—"

"Remember that teacher's daughter? Miss what-was-her-name?"

"Let's not talk about that."

"Where'd she go?"

"The daughter? No one knows, God rest her soul."

"For a while, I was scared the kids would find her somewhere—"

"It was so long ago—"

"I said I don't like to talk about that!"

"That was a hell of a fall."

"Poor girl."

"I don't know, she's not fooling me with this act."

Mia rubs a thumb across her sneakers. Her expression realigns. She shoves the sunglasses on her face. She pulls at her ponytail and her hair springs loose and huge. She stands up. She does not look at Eddie or at anyone as she struts out of the mall. The crowd parts before her. We climb onto our booth table to brandish our still and loyal faces to her, but she does not look over to us once. She marches past a family entering through the automatic doors, sending a toddler tumbling, and we watch as she disappears into the whiteness of a bare Florida afternoon. We do not hesitate. We leap off the table and sprint in her shadow toward the ascendant light.

BRITNEY

look in the mirror. I stick on my black bow tie, adjust it. It looks like I am presenting my head as a gift. I have worn this uniform five nights a week for almost five years. I am a waitress for the most exclusive catering company in the city. I have held trays up to CEOs, senators, billionaires, artists. I don't remember a single one of their faces.

My mother likes my bow tie, my black slacks. My uniform does nothing for my figure. It broadens my shoulders, flattens the waves of my breasts, my waist, my hips into a straight line. A body with no life in it.

"No trouble," my mother wrote, approvingly, when she asked to see a picture of me in it a long time ago.

My mother is always worried about trouble. She only calls me when the sun goes down. My mother's job is to protect me and so she believes she only needs to speak to me when it gets dark. She asks for the addresses of my jobs, the hotels and the conference centers, the ballrooms, the estates, the country houses, the beach cottages. I make up names and numbers to satisfy her. When I visited her last Thanksgiving, I found dozens of scraps of paper under a cushion on the couch, full of years of my light, impressive lies.

The Feenbody Hotel. North Hampton Avenue. Rockaway Plaza. The Tysky Gallery. The Golden Egg.

I could give her the real names, but I am afraid of her looking them up and calling if she decides to have her third glass of wine and becomes convinced I am going to die that night.

I often receive voicemails from her. I listen to them as I walk the blocks home. I am never scared. My mother talks about the dark like I imagined it when I was a child, that noisy, Floridian darkness, voiced by cicadas and thick as flesh. A true darkness. In the city, the sky never blackens. Sometimes it looks slightly burnt. My mother and I have traded places since I have grown up. We have bartered our fear. She pretends to be afraid and I pretend to be fearless. She sends me money for taxis and makes me promise never to walk home. I use the money to buy eggs and pancakes in all-night diners, sometimes keys of cocaine from my coworkers.

Sometimes I like to punish myself. Or sometimes I like to put myself in situations just to see how my body will react. I used to be curious about other people but now I am curious about myself. I often feel like I am living my life three feet to the left of my body. I let her live her life over there while I watch her. I prefer to be empty and cavernous.

I have not seen his face since the court case. Christian came to stay when it started. We thought maybe we should watch it on TV. Our takeout congealed on the table, untouched, as we chugged beers like we were watching a football game. We only lasted ten minutes. We turned it off and went out, took so many shots that we threw up side by side in an alley by midnight. We got pizza and then went out dancing. I told Christian to stay forever. I told him he didn't have to pay rent, just stay with me, always, please. We drank more. I got in a fight with a guy in the smoking area who told me I had a nice ass. Christian made out with the DJ. We screamed at each other in the taxi home for leaving each other, then woke up spooning. I still speak to him every day, but he never came back to visit, and the court case never went anywhere, either, as far as I've seen.

I look down at the mark on my thigh. I have hung my black slacks on the shower rail while my roommate showers so the steam takes out the creases. I look ridiculous, in my underwear and white work shirt and bow tie, my top bun so tight my eyebrows are cinched upward.

My mother says I've had the mark since birth, she insists on it. Once in high school I came home so drunk I cried and told her about him, about the house. She was silent until I said, about the mark, how it couldn't be true but I felt he had given it to me somehow.

"I gave that to you," she said. "It's a birthmark."

I had never heard her sound so angry.

"I gave that to you," she said.

We didn't talk about it again until I mentioned I was going to work at his art opening.

"You're crazy," she said. "Why would you do that to yourself?"

"He's not going to be there," I said. "I asked."

"Don't look back, never look back," she said. "It's the only way forward."

She always says this, but I know what's behind me. It's what is in front that scares me. It could be anything. It could easily be worse.

My roommate comes in holding my pants from the shower. There are still creases in them and now they are damp. She hands them to me. We have lived together long enough now that we have become a symbiotic organism. Slowly, boundaries have dissolved. We eat cereal at the sink in our underwear. We never close the door when we pee. Our periods are synced. When we watch TV together in one of our beds, our stomachs seem to talk to each other as our food digests, gurgling back and forth. We often fall asleep in the same bed. I have never liked to sleep alone. I don't like to be the only alive thing in a room. It makes me feel outnumbered.

I pull on the pants.

"Are you sure you want to go?" she says.

I wish I had never told her. It was when we first became friends, fellow waitresses, both a bottle down after work, cocaine working in our bowels, making us shit out our respective traumas. I hated doing it. When I was drunk or high, I couldn't step out of my body. I was a snotty, bloody mess like everyone else. I don't remember what she told me about herself. Obviously I didn't find it too interesting.

"I'm curious," I say.

Her mouth is consciously sympathetic, like the inflated downturned lips of a sad clown. I suddenly want to hit her, but the thought of hitting her is enough. Those lips bursting. Blood like lipstick. Her eyes wander toward my clenched fists. I think that she might want me to hit her, so she could call her boyfriend and tell him about my psychotic break.

"I think she's in love with me," she would whisper, somewhat hopefully, into her pillow.

"Have a good night?" she says, her voice a question mark. I leave.

I take the train downtown to the gallery. A group of teen-age boys eat slices of pizza. One's cheese slides off onto the dull floor, and the rest dare him to pick it up and eat it. He does and they all scream. A grandma knits across from me. A few women seek my eyes in solidarity of judgment but I close them. I look safe, a girl in a uniform. Women are always looking at me. I have an effect on them. I am broad, unfeminine, I awaken no envy, no nostalgia, no what-could-have-been. I don't know what they think I can do for them. I often have the urge to kiss these women, to rise up and plant my face onto theirs, women with wedding rings and gray hair, women with mascara stains and seeds in their teeth. A smack, a slap, a slammed door of a kiss. The kind of kiss that wakes you up and leaves you.

I've never trusted artists. They're so sleazy it almost makes me laugh.

As a waitress, I've met enough of them to know they are all the same. The first person I ever loved was a dancer. We met in a fast-food line at 4:00 a.m., a few weeks after I moved away from home. He was compact and small and I am tall and wide. I've always liked to hold people and he liked to be held. He never danced in front of me but he asked me to dance sometimes when we went to bed, playing pop songs I liked. I was eighteen, I loved to dance, I jumped over him on the bed, knocking myself against the walls, eager to please him.

Before we broke up, he choreographed a solo piece for his school. I was excited. I went alone, I didn't know anyone else in the city. He looked gorgeous on stage, curled in a white ball of light. His muscles looked carved. I was so turned on I wanted to eat him with my bare hands, like a cake. Then he started. He began in front of a mirror. Someone offstage pushed a cart out toward him. He donned a white shirt and a bow tie. A silhouette of a city appeared behind him, the traveling light of a subway car. He walked in an absurd way, his shoulders hunched, his large strides almost circles. He pirouetted and a table full of food and wineglasses was rolled out to him, knocking him in the ass. He mimed shock, as if bursting out of a reverie, and the audience laughed. He put four plates full of food on his arms, balanced from his wrist to his elbow, and then staggered around, dropping them all on the floor. He drew ten wineglasses into his balletically curled fingers. I had taught him these tricks, ones I'd known since bussing in high school. Then he started to dance badly, the glasses cracking, knocking against one another in his fingers, the food smudging all over the floor beneath his feet. He looked insane, turning circles, his hands clenching to fists as the glasses dropped to the ground. I wanted to nudge the person next to me. I wanted to be rude. What is this guy doing! I wanted to say. Some people started to chuckle. I laughed, too, a mean, loud laugh. I had always thought there was something beautiful about the way I danced. The girls had always made me feel that way. The way they watched me dance! The way they danced with me, the way we rippled away from one another! I couldn't believe how stupid he looked. I left. He still calls me sometimes. For a long time, I didn't understand why, but now I think that to humiliate a woman is the only way some men know how to love one.

The gallery is empty when I arrive. I hate working at these kinds of events. Too many people crammed into a small room. And all the whiteness. Light that shows everyone too clearly.

His name is painted onto the front glass wall in a trendy font. The name that signed my mother's paychecks for years.

Nathan is at the bar. I like Nathan. He has high hips, high cheekbones. "I was born to flirt," he told me once. And it is true, he does not even have to try. There is something devilish about him, his bones so close to the surface, his eyes shiny but metallic, cold. I would love to be cold but it is difficult for a woman. People seem to see warmth in me even when I offer none. Maybe if I was thinner it would be easier, but it seems to me sometimes that a woman with flesh is a woman who must always be grateful. People don't hesitate around me. I am always being asked for favors, and causing offense when I say no.

Nathan tried this at first. He asked me to close down the bar while he cashed up. Closing down the bar was a ten-step job, the accounts a one-step, sit-down ordeal you could do while drinking. When I said no, he smiled guiltily, poured me a whisky, and hauled out the trash.

He hands me a whisky now, and I start cutting the fruit.

I look at the photographs on the walls. Huge, stretched canvases. They are so in focus they make my head hurt. They are boring and badly lit.

The series is called "Doors."

There are European doors in flaking pastels, English doors at the seaside, bright-red doors covered in Chinese characters, the rounded doors of a mosque, revolving glass doors, doors ajar, half-broken doors, a hotel hallway of identical doors, the dull white doors of a hospital, door after door after door.

"I hate photos without people," says Nathan. He squints at the doors. "These make me nervous."

I pour another whisky and he raises a singular, slick eyebrow.

"They piss me off," I say, and drink.

We are only responsible for the drinks. Another caterer is serving food, which makes the floor so full it is almost impossible to navigate. Blond waitresses swerve through the crowd like tiny sharks. I hear the squeak of their voices announcing their offerings: monkfish livers, kohlrabi, truffled deviled eggs. I hijack a few when I go to the bathroom and put them all into my mouth together in the stall. It's hard to swallow. I come out, and a woman is waiting, clad in velvet, chunks of turquoise pegged onto her ears. "They let the staff use the toilets?" she says to no one. She goes into the stall I've vacated and I hope I peed on the seat. I smile at myself in the mirror, the food stuffed to my gums. Some of the mush falls into the white sink. I don't wash my hands.

I circulate with flutes of champagne, holding the tray on the pads of my fingers, lowering it only when necessary to avoid crashes. I enjoy making them reach for the drinks, I enjoy making them look at me. This is out of character. Normally, I like the numbness, the invisibility of waitressing. But tonight I meet their eyes. They look away immediately but I do not blink.

A man winds his arm around my waist and pinches my hip bone. His speech doesn't flinch or falter, and he continues his smooth way to a punch line as the two women beside him laugh. They notice, as women notice everything, but women are as good at ignoring things as they are at understanding them.

Another man asks for a neat whisky. I fill it with ice because I want to make someone angry. He turns purple when I present it to him, recoils when I pretend not to notice and knock the cold glass against his hand.

My heart feels like a solid dead thing. I can't even feel it beating. I feel the old stirring in my gut, to light a match and play with the flame.

I stand at the bar and look at the warm swirl of bodies, prodded and injected and polished by money. The women look oiled. The men look dry. They talk to each other but their eyes move all around the room, scanning for an exit. Laughs scatter competitively throughout the crowd, increasing in length and volume until they dissolve, and then it starts again, like a wave at a baseball game.

I wonder what they know.

I suspect they know everything.

I hate that he picked something as obvious as a door.

I pick up a fresh tray from the bar.

"Are you okay?" asks Nathan.

I move to the center of the floor.

A dozen claws lift up toward my tray.

I look up at the glasses full of gold.

The blond heads swim around me.

It is a dance as good as any other.

It takes the tiniest effort to cause significant damage, or at least a lot of noise.

I have always loved breaking glass. It is so easy to do that it is like the glass wants to break. It wants to be free. It wants to be a thousand flecks of shrieking glitter, announcing an entrance, a star of the show.

People scream as the tray falls from my hand. They throw up their bejeweled fingers to protect their eyes from the splinters of glass. The champagne creates a yellow puddle in the middle of the shining floor, like dog piss.

The men and the women and the waitresses back away from me like I am something rabid. They look like they expect me to cry. I almost do. I think about laughing, too, but in the end, I do neither. I toe the yellow liquid wider with my sneaker. The silence is gorgeous. It ripples out of me like the most brilliant piece of art.

The mall parking lot looks spectacular, vast and white-tipped, like an ocean that we are not afraid of because we know exactly what it is. The light rains down upon it, picking up the chrome on the car hubcaps, whiting out the side mirrors and the tinted windows, beaming off the sunroofs, causing the faint scent in the air of scorched flesh as the bugs burn in the crevices of the windshields. We run. The light seems to cheer us on, cheer on all humans in their capacity, if nothing else, to make mean and shiny things. The dogs stuck in the back seats of the cars force their jaws into the thin free space of the left-open windows. They begin to bark as we fly by, harmonizing our calls of her name.

"Mia!"

"Mia!"

"Mia!"

We feel like men in every movie our moms watch.

We are halfway across the lot by the time we hear her crying, and we love her for this. Of course, she cannot wave or call out to us. We have to find her and save her. We feel inflated with purpose.

We find her in a dark wedge of shadow between a pickup and a Ford Focus, scratching at the white line that marks the parking space. She is hunched over, but she looks up as we darken her further with our shadow. We see ourselves in her glasses, our outlines jostling, one clumsy, wavering creature. She looks at us like she does not know us. We do not know what to do next except watch her.

Leila elbows her way to the front, even though she is the slowest runner and arrived last. She crouches on her big bare feet and peers at Mia, or herself in Mia's sunglasses. Then she leans over and kisses her on the lips.

We feel a crackle between us. We close our eyes because we want the kiss to belong to all of us, but we also know that it does not. We feel glass spring up between us and where Leila and Mia sit, kissing. We know we can break the glass in a shower over their heads if we want to. We clench our fists.

Leila breaks free and rocks back on her heels. She hugs her knees and rests her head on them.

In the quiet, the kiss seems to shrivel in the air like a popped balloon.

We cannot look at Leila or each other. We cross our arms over our chests. We wait for the kiss to be handed back to us like our discarded shirts on the basketball court.

Mia moves her head slowly between each of us. She takes the time to fill her sunglasses up with each of our faces. We feel separated and weird. Then she turns back to Leila and sticks out her tongue. She takes a yellow clump from its tip and forces it between Leila's closed lips. Dry flakes fall and we think that Leila does not use enough ChapStick and was probably disgusting to kiss. Leila takes a hesitant chew.

Mia sits back on her ass. She opens her mouth as if to speak or scream or vomit. Something seems to be rising in her that is heavy and foul, direct from the gut. It takes us a second to translate the sound that comes out of her mouth because we have never heard a sound like it before. It is high-pitched and rough and reminds us of when Hazel had an asthma attack.

"I think she's laughing," says Leila.

We are relieved Leila is still going to narrate the world for us even if she has betrayed us and been alone. We nod.

"Oh!" says Jody.

"Duh!" says Britney.

Mia laughs so hard she falls over onto the asphalt. Her cheek scrapes against the rough black surface and her sunglasses fall down to the end of her nose, revealing that her eyes are dry. We realize that she is not crying. We suddenly doubt she ever was. We look at Leila. We are suspicious. The false tears seem like a trap, like the traps our mothers set when they dance for men. We wriggle in the wet ropes she's wrapped around us. Our soft hearts thump and we think of the girls we broke on Leila's blog with our promises of love.

"Where is she?" says Mia, and collapses in laughter again. "She thinks she can run away from me!" She keeps laughing. We do not know what else to do except wait for her to stop.

•

It takes her a long time. The sun slaps our skin. We want to go back to the mall and see Eddie, but we feel guilty for leaving him. We feel we have betrayed him. We have betrayed Sammy. We have fallen under Mia's spell and now we cannot escape it.

"Let's go to my house," she says. "You stay with me." She takes Leila by the hand. We scuttle behind them because we do not know how to sever ourselves in a clean or dignified way. We will cling to Leila until she hangs to us by a single fiber and there is blood and bone all over us.

Christian tries first. He wriggles as close to them as he can without forcing his way between them.

"This town's roadkill," he says. He can barely speak. "I can't wait for L.A."

Mia does not seem to hear him. Leila does not look around. He slinks back between us. We take his hands but they slip through ours, and he puts them in his pockets.

We follow. We try to remember how we used to walk when we were only ourselves but we cannot. We take a stride and it is absurd, like how we walk in the chorus of the school musical when we are jovial villagers. We take another step but it is too short and we lurch forward, almost knocking our heads between Mia and Leila's shoulder blades. Mia turns around to look at us and we freeze. We remember the game our grandmas used to play with us, when we crept up behind them to bang on their butt cheeks before they noticed, spun around, and roared at us like wolves. We stay still. We hope she will roar. We are in the mood for a roar.

"You are so funny," says Mia. She looks at Leila. "Aren't they so funny?"

Leila jerks her head. It could be a nod or a shake. Britney hovers a little behind us, and we hear the low beginning of a bark in her throat, the sound she makes before she breaks something or starts to dance.

"You're like dogs still waiting at the pound," says Mia. She pushes her sunglasses up, widens her eyes until they start to water. She looks at us like she wants to be loved. Then she laughs and puts her sunglasses back on.

We are embarrassed. We feel our faces turn to fur. Bars descend before our eyes, and Mia and Leila look giant to us, looking down on us to judge our possible place in their pretty lives. We are furious at the same time as we would do anything to be chosen, wag our tails, look sad, cry, play dead.

"Don't worry," says Mia. "I'm a dog, too."

She opens her mouth and produces a bark so realistic that the dogs trapped in the hot cars begin to cry and howl with longing. We move closer to her, but she turns back to Leila. We stop, bumping into one another, banging shoulders. We want to be the girls at the front, the next ones to be picked. Mia lifts her long nail and moves it toward Leila's face. Leila's eyes cross, trying to keep the nail in focus. We hold our breath, but then Mia softens, takes a strand of Leila's dark hair, and tucks it behind one of her ears.

"You know, you're really pretty," says Mia. "You should model or something."

It is so much better in real life than when we had practiced saying this line to one another, sitting in a circle at lunch or on the apartment's playground, taking turns to choose one another and be chosen, brandishing our claws of painted nails and whispering:

"You know, you're so pretty."

"You're perfect for this movie."

"You have to make out with him in one scene!"

"Pack your bags, sweetie."

"You are so crazy beautiful."

"No one's ever told you that?"

We could pack our mom's suitcases in five minutes. For the end of the game, we dragged them to the curb and then took turns pretending to be our mothers, wrapping our arms around one another's legs, sinking to our knees, and wailing, "How could you leave me?"

We shook one another off, our eyes starry.

"Mom, this is a really big deal for me."

But we stopped playing this summer. None of us played fair. We stopped taking turns and none of us wanted to be our mothers or the agent. All of us wanted to be the newly discovered star.

"You're so pretty you're so pretty you're so pretty." We said it very fast so no one could butt in. We swatted at one another with our nails. We left scratches across one another's cheeks. Our voices turned hoarse. Hazel had her asthma attack.

Leila smiles. "I've thought about modeling some, I guess," she says.

"Sure, your mirror's thought about it, right?" says Mia.

They both laugh.

We want to throw up.

We cannot believe Leila has become pretty without us noticing, but we realize we have never really looked at her. We assumed she belonged to us so wholly that we had forgotten to.

We look now.

Her eyes are brown with small flecks of gold. We notice that she has the first hints of cheekbones to scaffold her beauty, holding it up to the light.

Britney spits onto the tarmac. We are angry, too. We are sure Leila is hoarding spells and potions, beauty secrets enmeshed in some other Internet we do not have access to.

Mia's phone rings. She lifts it to her ear.

"What do you want?" she says. She listens.

"I'll be at the lake," she says. "I'm with the girls."

She hangs up.

"Eddie got a plane ticket to L.A," she says.

We shiver with excitement. We see Eddie dragging along a full suitcase and wonder if we can zip ourselves inside it. Plane tickets are only for kids destined for lives we can barely taste, lives far bigger than local car dealership commercials or mall catwalk shows for prom dresses. A plane ticket is the promise of real fame, glorious, shining, terrifying fame. Fame that lives in big white-walled houses and movies set in big white-walled houses.

"When's he leaving?" Leila squeaks.

"Tomorrow," says Mia. She rolls her eyes. "It's nice, you know. Like a feel-good story. To see people like him do okay. You have to have a sob story, my mom says. He probably got up there and cried about Sammy going missing."

We look at one another. Eddie never sobs, we think. Eddie was born happy.

Leila plays with her ear lobes.

Christian bites his thumb.

Britney spits again.

We should speak, we think, to save his beauty from blasphemy, but seconds pass and we do not. We are jealous and feel small. We do not want him to leave. Our hearts feel husky, like cicada shells. We wait for them to flap or thump or wriggle, for a worm of life to sprout from them, but they keep their same dull obedient beat.

"Are you with me, girls?" says Mia. She takes a stack of Star Search cards from her back pocket and starts to shuffle them. We look at them hungrily and nod.

We follow Mia and Leila through town. They link arms and whisper. We do not sing or run or play. We whisper, too, and force ourselves to laugh loudly even though we are not saying anything funny. The fake laughs hurt our faces. We feel waves of discontent float and fall softly over us. We have always been afraid of being alone but we thought we knew the cure: being together. Now we are together and we still feel alone. It is terrible and we grab one another, denying this soft sadness that is like our mothers'. We tug Christian's hands from his pockets, we link our pinkie fingers, lean on one another's shoulders, and wrap our arms around one another's waists.

Walking along the highway, we pass the water park we always go to in the summer, where our backs bleed from the chinks between the plastic sections of the slides. The go-kart place pumps out gray gas. The World's Tallest Swing Ride hangs empty, the neon lights along the legs muted, lit only by bleaching sunlight. A boy died on it a few weeks ago. It was on the news, he fell off it from three hundred feet. They said it was a pre-existing heart condition, but they always say it is a pre-existing heart condition or a routine safety check gone wrong. That was what they said when the old lady slipped beneath the bar on the superhero roller coaster and landed in the lake below, when the boy got his leg stuck in an electric track on the alien ride and had to have it amputated, when the man got electrocuted when he went overboard on a boat and met the animatronic shark beneath the water.

The cars are stuck along the road and we pass the cops parked before the highway exit, leaning into windows and popping open trunks, shining lights into dark corners.

We are so hot that the world starts to blur, the atoms of the universe are fusing. We are relieved when we see Falls Landing, but Mia leads us past it, over the construction site, and down toward the lake. We pause at some abandoned trash cans from the search party, looking for water bottles, but when we reach them there is only melted ice left, brown and warm as old coffee.

There are a couple of women dotted around, crouched outside of steaming tents, returning from the audition. Another woman stands by the white wall holding a shovel, her forehead glistening with sweat, a dirt trench dug all the way from the road.

"Seen anything, girls?" she calls out.

We shake our heads, look shyly at our feet.

We hear music coming from the large white tent and scurry toward it. The flaps have been rolled down. We creep after Mia and Leila and lie in a row on our bellies, lift the white flaps to peer under and inside. Women lounge across the shaded grass, fanning themselves with rolled-up missing posters. There are the church women, but we are surprised to see Leila's and Christian's moms, too, their eyes silly and hopeful, their legs crisscrossed. They are all staring toward the front of the tent, where Sammy's dad sits on a low pallet, his big hands splayed over his knees, his eyes closed. Kneeling on the edge of the pallet is Sammy's mom, her face hidden within the sheets of her hair. Their t-shirts are creased. The angel wings have melted into glittery streams over Sammy's face.

"Where's my angel?" says Sammy's dad.

Britney makes a low buzzing sound. A few of the women in front of her, their eyes closed, flap their hands by their heads. We giggle softly.

After Sammy had her birthday party, we looked for her on the Internet. We were hoping for a blog, a diary, but we found nothing. Eventually, we looked at her dad's preacher website. We skipped and skipped until we found a video of Sammy. "Little Girl Hears Angel Voices." It had over a million views. In the video, Sammy was only a little kid. She sat on the floor playing with a stuffed toy dog and scratching at her ears.

"What's in your ears, baby?" her mom said from behind the camera.

"Scratch," said Sammy.

"What do you hear?"

"Wings," she said.

"Whose wings?"

"En-gels, en-gels," she said.

Her dad came into the shot. He gave her a piece of

paper and asked her to draw what was in her ear. She drew the angels we were taught to recognize in kindergarten, white girls with two squiggles of blonde hair and two blobs of blue for eyes, a huge triangle for a body. It was Leila's mom who found us watching on her computer and told us what really happened.

"You know Sammy Liu-Lou?" we said, shocked.

"I know about her," she said. "You don't forget a story like that. Those sure weren't angel wings."

We shivered.

"Bad en-gels!" Sammy said in the video.

Leila's mom told us the angels turned out to be a single baby wasp that had crawled into Sammy's ear while she slept, then tried to escape in the morning.

"Her daddy was all set for *Good Morning America* and then those angels blew up her ear," she said. She laughed but the story terrified us. A loose wasp could send a whole crowd of apartment kids running toward the lesser perils of the highway or the lake.

When her dad looks up, he seems to meet our eyes. Britney stops buzzing.

"Where is she?" he says. His voice is sad and we do not like sadness. We think of him imagining his daughter was talking to God, and how he felt when a baby wasp crawled out of her ear instead. We drop the flaps of the tent and roll away out of sight. It is only then that we notice Mia and Leila are gone.

•

We search. We are wild with loss. We feel our last sinew with Leila stretch and strain, and it feels like we are losing a part of our bodies, something key to our function, like a heart or a bladder.

"They're down there," says Britney. We look. A swoop of screams reaches us from the theme parks. We see smoke from the fertilizer factory, coughs of dark clouds. Britney points closer to the lake near the dock. We see the two girls shimmering in the heat like a mirage. Their backs are turned to us.

The jealousy we have felt since we first saw Mia and Sammy give a card to another girl feels heavy in our stomachs, a pool of thick and sticky gasoline. We are scared that with one false move, one misstep, we will implode.

We watch their figures, so close, in the pose of secrets. We could scream but we do not. We do what we always do and we watch.

Our jealousy changes the longer we are still. It turns from hot and tender to cold and hard, like when we burn our fingers on the stove and have to calm them under our tongues. Our bodies react to soothe our souls from pain as well as our skin.

We are ugly, we think.

We knew this already.

We are unwanted, we think.

We knew this already.

Britney leads us. She crouches down on her hands and knees and we crawl down to the dock. We lie flat on our bellies, so we are less visible, though we realize it does not matter. They are not looking at us and have never looked at us. No one looks at us and this gives us a brutal power.

Our mothers call us brutes when they want us to feel bad. It is what they call men they do not like, like our dads.

They called us brutes when we dared Hazel to jump off the banyan into the shallow end of the pool. She broke her leg and we think that one is still shorter than the other. In photos, she always has to slouch.

They called us brutes when we told Christian he shouldn't be afraid to wear Britney's skirt to school in sixth grade, and some high school boys put him in a trash can.

They called us brutes when we broke the bathroom mirror to scare Leila after we called on the devil three times and pretended to be possessed.

They called us brutes every time they found us setting fire to ant nests on the playground, which we swore were built on Britney's dad's blood.

They called us brutes when we knocked the baby birds from the banyan branches into the paws of the stray cats. We did not want to hear the chicks squeaking for mothers that the cats had already brought us dead as gifts.

They called us brutes the summer we got obsessed with

lizards and they found the bodies beneath our beds, the tails kept in separate Ziploc bags marked with how long they kept moving after we pulled them off. We had competitions and if we won, we kept the tails as trophies.

They called us brutes when we got salmonella after we ate a whole bowl of raw brownie mix.

They called us brutes when Jody's tampon fell out in the pool and we all got kicked out for a day so it could be cleaned.

They called us brutes when we told them their boyfriends were perverts, which they were.

They called us brutes when we pierced Christian's ear with a paper clip and an orange, and when the stud got stuck in his ear, we tried to yank it out with pliers and his earlobe split in two.

They called us brutes when we got tired of being called brutes and collected dead wasps with their stingers still in, slipped them into their work Crocs, the coin sections of their purses.

"Brutes! How can you girls be such brutes?"

They cried. We cried, too, because we felt they were saying we were wrong. We felt foul and fatherly and frightened of ourselves. We tried to make ourselves small. We were coiled up but we were not broken. And we knew our mothers' idea of goodness was not measured by morals but by how much noise we made. And we quickly grew tired of trying to be good in their way.

"You don't have to do anything," we hear Mia say at the edge of the lake.

"Have you done it?" says Leila.

"Sure," says Mia. "You just stand there."

"What about the pictures?"

"They don't have your face in them. You check. And you get free classes or you can take the two hundred. Whatever you want."

Leila takes a small step away from her. She is closer to the lake than we ever normally dare go.

"You're lucky," says Mia. "I don't ask just anybody."

"I know," says Leila.

"If you don't want to, it's no big deal," says Mia. She takes a step toward Leila, closing the space between them. The edge of the lake is black and still, brushing at Leila's heels.

"I don't want to," says Leila.

"Are you scared? It's not scary. It's just, like, a job."

"No," says Leila. "I just don't wanna do it."

Leila stands up straighter, but before she reaches the height of Mia's sunglasses, Mia reaches out and pushes her toward the water. It is a small shove, tiny, barely a push, but the timing is fated. Mia hits Leila just as she is rising back to the bank, and she is caught in between, unbalanced. Leila's arms windmill and she falls back. She swings her arms wide across the water as if grabbing its surface will save her. Her mouth opens but no sound comes out. It is full of black water. There is hardly any splash, no rush of bubbles. The water seems to part beneath her. It opens like a door if a door were to open and then immediately disappear.

"Leila," we whisper.

A lie.

We do not whisper. We lie still and do nothing. We think our own thoughts. It reminds us of the summer when Britney's grandmother died. We were at her house for a sleepover. When her mother got the call, she started to cry on the couch, rocking back and forth, and we did not know what to do but watch her. She seemed crazy. "My mother is dead!" she kept hissing. It seemed false and complicated to us, this multiplication of mothers. Our mothers could not also be daughters, just as we would never be mothers. Our heads hurt from figuring it out while Britney's mom sobbed and we watched her. The rest of our mothers arrived in a flock, they embraced Britney's mother, they cried with her, they seemed to know exactly what to do. "Come hug your mamas!" they cried, rushing around, fetching wine, sweet things, soft things, but we did not want to join in. We slunk back and they looked at us like we were strangers. We pushed our little sisters and brothers forward and our mothers held them instead.

Britney turns her head to us in the grass.

"Maybe she's being like the lake boy," she whispers.

We have been told since birth never to go near the lake, and it is the only rule no one is tempted to disobey. Our mothers used the monster to threaten us. Go to bed or we'll leave you on the dock in the dark. Stop hitting your sister or we'll put you in a boat while you're sleeping. Even the boys who want to show they are fearless won't stick a toe in the lake, feigning disinterest and saying it's too full of piss and shit. Not because of any dumb monster stories, they say, and we laugh like we believe them, then spend our nights shivering in our sleep, sure the monster knows it was us who laughed at it.

Our little brothers and sisters are scared of the monster, too, but they are too young and have not yet learned to lie. They hear the monster's claws scratching the water pipes, they feel the gasp of its close breath when they blink in the tub. They can smell its stink, like wet laundry, and know it's in the room, watching, waiting for them to fall asleep. That is when they crawl into our beds, and we do not mind, because we feel brave when we pretend we are brave.

We have only seen one person enter the lake before Leila. We caught him in our binoculars just before sunset a few weeks before Sammy went missing. We waited for Eddie to bring around his ladder. We were early, excited to watch. We held the hope of every summer in history inside of us, that soon we would have someone to sneak out for in the loud sticky nights, that soon there would be someone who'd whisper in our ears, bring us snacks, and hold us on a dirty mattress.

We had our binoculars focused on the white wall, trying to pinpoint exactly where Sammy normally rose up, when we noticed a boy creeping around the corner, like he'd just come out of the Falls Landing gate. It was the golden hour, the light softened around the edges, illuminating the sand flies and air particles into an atmosphere of subtle glitter. The boy was not yet the lake boy. He was just a boy. He was not anyone we knew, though he looked around our age. He was alone. We watched as he picked his way over the construction site. He sat on the show home step for a while. He wriggled his hand into a hole in the wonky step. He pulled out dead palmetto bugs, roaches, woodlice. He retrieved each shell one by one, then lined them up on his thumb. He flicked the shells farther and farther, squinting to see how far they traveled. Then he took a plastic gun out of his pocket, one we recognized from the dollar store, made of clear neon plastic. We could see the liquid inside was dark as lake water. He aimed the gun into the hole in the step, sprayed, then took a matchbox from his pocket, lit a match, and threw it in. A small puffy flame burst out and he warmed his hands over it. Then he looked out toward the lake.

The sky turned fleshy with sunset. Shadows grew long and sharp across the construction site. Car headlights bloomed on the highway.

Soon the show home step caught the dark. He stretched and his t-shirt rose up, revealing a sparse line of hair to his belly button, a complicated whorl we longed to fill with ink and stamp on our wrists like a temporary tattoo.

We took a long, thirsty look at him as he moved toward the lake. He walked like a roach, still and then suddenly at speed. He did not take his eyes from his feet so we could not catch their color, but his feet were a revelation to us. He was not wearing shoes, and his feet were as determinedly damaged as ours. His nails were so pointed we thought he must sharpen them himself with a file. The buildup of dead skin on his heels was so impressive that he tottered like our mothers in their wedge sandals.

He stood by the lake as the sky ripped itself up around him. Strips of it seemed to land and float on the lake's surface, great hunks of pink sky.

Then he turned. He stared right up at our windows. We could not believe it. Did he know we were there? No one had ever looked at us before.

We wanted to live inside his look forever, but he turned back to the lake. He rubbed his hands together and started to undress. He took off his t-shirt, his pants. His boxers were baby blue and billowed around his bony thighs like a miniskirt. He was tanned as though sprayed with orange luminescence. We stared at his body as he gingerly tiptoed, then bent, then lowered himself beneath the glassy surface of the water. He swam out a few feet, his head perched above the surface like a dog. His strokes made pink wings across the water.

Then he flipped onto his back, turned to us again. We waved, imagining our faces bathed in the beautiful light. We wondered if we should go down to join him.

But suddenly he started to thrash, as though he were being drowned.

We lowered our hands to our hair, unsure. We saw him taking gulps of air, kicking his legs, smashing his arms from one side to the other. We were shocked. We could not have been more surprised if we saw an old man in red smash through our glass doors in December, or woke up to see a tiny winged woman shaking a sack full of teeth. We felt our stories hit us with a swift and powerful certainty, that the stories we told were not just stories, but creatures, both dangerous and true.

We could save him, we thought. We could run down and pull him from the monster's mouth, and he would love us like heroes. We could get our picture in the school newsletter.

But we were scared. We were not meant to be watching.

And we were powerful. We could preserve this moment perfectly, powerful with a secret, a secret that seemed ancient, like something from the Bible or a story our mothers told us to go to sleep. The school newsletter seemed shallow in comparison.

We watched the strange orange boy splash for ten

minutes, and dip below the water for one. We knew Sammy
and Eddie would be arriving soon. We had time to rehearse
our stories as we watched the lake digest him. We had them
perfect by the time we felt he was sunk.

"That was so sad about that boy," we would say.

"He was hot!" we would say.

"We can't believe no one saw anything," we would say.

Maybe we would even manage to cry, and our mothers
would hold us to their chests and comfort us. They would
tell us to be careful, and to never go near the water because
they could not live without us. And we would promise.

We blinked our eyes clean when he bobbed up again,
spitting water. He swam leisurely back to the grass. He
looked up at our windows and we quickly hid.

We were ashamed.

We were ravenous.

We peeked. He lay in the grass, his orange chest pumping. Our breath misted the window and we had to keep
moving our binoculars to find a clear spot. He lay there
until the sunset was over, and then, holding his clothes under his armpits, he traveled back along the wall. We remembered Sammy and flicked our lenses back to its cusp.
We were surprised to see she was already there, kicking her
heels very fast against it. When the lake boy shuffled past,
she tilted her head back and threw out a spit bullet, but it
missed him, and he did not look up at her once.

When he disappeared inside Falls Landing, Sammy

hopped off the wall and disappeared, too, even though we saw Eddie was already retrieving his ladder from Britney's mom's boyfriend's truck. We watched as Eddie crossed the construction site and stood beneath her vacated spot, tapping the ladder against the wall as though calling her. She was a little late, but eventually she returned, and we watched as she flew down into his arms, as quickly as she had done every time before.

We did not speak about the lake or the boy too often. When the fires started around town, we followed them with interest, picking up codes in his chosen places like we did with Sammy and Mia and their nail polish. What did it mean to burn the dumpster outside of the pet store? What did it mean to burn down the flower shop of the florist who had run off to New York with the school principal? What did it mean to burn down the top of the Styrofoam volcano at the crazy golf course that stretched over the highway?

We did not know who he was. We had not seen him again, and we were scared to ruin him with words.

When we couldn't resist remembering him, we called him the lake boy.

"I wonder what the lake boy's doing," one of us would say, and it worked like an incantation, we were instantly lost in powerful, pastel dreams.

10

Watching the still water, familiar excuses travel telepathically between us, allowing Leila to disappear.

She betrayed us by leaving us, we think.

She betrayed us with that scabby kiss.

She betrayed us with her pretty hair.

We do not cry out. We do not call for help. We do not run to the shore and dive after her, lifting her in our arms, pumping her chest until she coughs up watery mud.

A second passes. Then another.

Mia backs away from the water. She turns and we wonder if she will run toward Falls Landing. We wonder if we can run after her.

We are not here, we think, we are not part of the scene. We have been cut out.

But then we hear a shout. We roll our heads in the grass and see Eddie, a shadow on the horizon of the highway, sprinting toward the lake. He does not seem to notice our bodies in the grass. He leaps over us like we are anthills. At the edge of the water, he does not hesitate. He raises his arms to a point and dives with barely a ripple into the water, sliding beneath its slimy surface.

We see Mia pause, look around, and then shuffle back to the water. We can see the top froth of Eddie's curls above the lake, and Mia holds her hand above them.

Leila is the worst one of us at holding her breath, we know.

Seconds can seem very long in silence. Of course, there is the distant drone of the highway, the static of radios, the hum of prayer and music from the tent, the occasional snatched laughter from the apartments. But silences can be universal and they can be specific between people, and there is a silence between us by the lake that is long with years none of us possess.

Eddie lifts Leila out of the water, the lake dripping from them, each dark water droplet punctured by the sun so it glitters. They stagger up the grass, and Eddie deposits Leila gently, holding her chin in his fingers. He pumps her chest, but her eyes are open when he leans over to breathe into her lips, and when he rises back up, she is smiling, her lovely eyes bright.

Eddie grins at her.

"You okay, sleepyhead?" he says. He ruffles her wet hair.

Leila coughs. She spits up some dark water, and it lands on Eddie's hand that holds her chin, a wobbling ball that looks more solid than a spit wad. Eddie drops her chin and wipes his hand off on the grass, grimacing. We watch the substance. We swear it seems to coalesce, forming the shape of a shiny black slug that starts to inch its way back toward the water. A laugh jerks out of us involuntarily and we have to stuff our faces into the grass. When we look up, the thing is gone. Leila's smile and eyes have dimmed. She bites her lip like she is about to cry.

Eddie looks at Mia, who is wiping her feet dry on the grass.

"You," he says. His voice seems to narrow. Mia looks around as if for someone to defend her, but Eddie is on her, his hands on her arms, and they half wrestle, her so wriggly he cannot seem to keep hold of her, and finally she raises her long nail and drags it across his cheekbone, turning the brown skin pink, then red. He drops her and steps farther away up the grass.

"Shit, Mia!" he says.

Leila wriggles in beside him. "Are you okay?" she asks.

"I'm supposed to leave tomorrow," he says. He thrusts his face toward Leila. "Is it gonna scar?"

Leila examines his face carefully. She peers so close we can see her breath moving the damp strands of his bangs, but he moves away before her lips make contact with his skin. He holds his hand to the bloody line and fingers it like we do with our zits.

Mia folds her nails into her palms and sighs.

"What are you doing pushing girls around all the time?" Eddie says. "I thought you knew where Sammy was."

"Maybe I do, maybe I don't," she says.

"You're so weird," he says. "It's like you think she belongs to you. She's not a toy."

"She doesn't belong to you, either."

"We belong together," says Eddie.

We swoon a little.

Mia looks out across the dark water, and we swear we feel a change in the air, some signal, some ancient order dispensed. We wonder if we have got it wrong, if it isn't just Eddie Mia loves, but Sammy, too. Eddie and Sammy are two, now, we think, and Mia is on the other side of the glass with us. We are all outside the warm diner of love, caught in snow swirls, looking in. We love Mia the way we once loved Sammy, because she isn't chosen and she refuses this fate. We know she will say something terrible. Sammy always stayed silent. We do not want silence now. We want to make powerful, mean noise.

"You know," says Mia, "you are so dumb. You are the dumbest boy I've ever known. I told Sammy you were, but she didn't believe me. I told her she'd get bored of you in two seconds. She didn't believe me, but I was right."

Dumb! We repeat in our heads. Dumb boy! We chuckle into the dirt.

"Where is she?" says Eddie.

"She was always so scared you were gonna find out," Mia says. "'He'll be so saaaad,' she said. 'You have to promise not to tell him ever.'"

"Where is she?" says Eddie.

"Sammy's been running after my brother all summer,"

she says. "You know my dad dumped him here because he tried to burn down his house?"

"Your brother?" says Eddie. "I've never seen him."

"He stays in his room all the time. He only comes out at night," says Mia. "He's a freak."

"You shouldn't talk about your brother like that," says Eddie.

"Aw," says Mia. "You're so cute. And dumb."

"He's not dumb!" whispers Leila. Neither of them look at her.

"My brother sprayed my dad's garage with gas and threw a match in," says Mia. She pauses. "His dog was in the garage. So they sent him here."

"What's he got to do with Sammy?" says Eddie.

"First day he got here, he comes in looking half-drowned, says he's been swimming in the lake. You should have seen her face. Like he'd come back from hell or something. And then he spat at her feet. Spat at the angel's feet! You know how she sleeps over at mine? She doesn't stay with me. She runs all over town with him and doesn't come back until morning."

The lake boy! we think. We rustle in the grass with excitement. We think of him and Sammy in the dark, in an empty parking lot stretched out like the ocean, their faces licked with light. Making small, beautiful fires.

"She was going to tell you before the audition," says

Mia. "Maybe she chickened out and ran off somewhere. She's a coward, you know. You think she's so deep because she's quiet. She's just scared. She tells me everything. More than you or my psycho brother. More than anyone."

Eddie's face is perfectly still. We are so unused to seeing him look sad that he looks like a stranger. He almost does not look beautiful.

"Are you seriously gonna cry?" says Mia. "She's really not gonna want you if you cry."

She seems surprised at how quickly he breaks, but we are not surprised. Eddie has no hardness. He has always been protected. Our mothers whispered scary stories above his pretty head, the same ones they threw in our faces. Eddie was always a blessed child, and to be always blessed and never blamed could make a child soft. He did not know how to lie or fight like we did.

We understand this but Mia does not.

We watch Eddie crumple, like a toddler feeling for the first time the dismissive swat of his mother's hand. We watch the possibility of being alone flood him with a fresh and unknown fear. We recognize it so deeply that we feel it, too, we feel it in our feet.

We do not usually feel fear in our feet.

They fizz.

We look over our shoulders. We notice we are wearing red shoes, though we do not own red shoes, and we never wear shoes anyway.

We have made another mistake.

We did not look where we lay.

The shoes become alive. Dark red ants shimmer across our skin, like pools of blood reflecting the lights of a fire. Every fiber in our feet stings. We feel the slow release of a thousand injections into our veins. The world whitens. We dissolve into a singular, ringing alarm. Our thoughts are erased into one simple scream. We are on fire, and so we run to water.

11

We run toward the lake with such single-minded determination that we trip, all in a row on the small sandy ring of the bank, flying into the water and belly-flopping over one another like lemmings. The force of our bodies slapping the water causes even those of us at the surface to sink, until we are tangled and confused, in a rush of bubbles and chaos. We feel the lake's resentment at this disturbance, and it seems to pull us down farther, and soon we are in a deep and black and still darkness. The water is cold. We have never felt a real chill in our lives, and the coldness of the water makes it seem weightless. We cannot rise to the surface. We toss and turn but we cannot tell what way is up or down. Fear floods us so wholly that we surrender to it and become strangely calm. There is no other feeling but fear so it fights against nothing and we are numb. Watery cold ropes twist around our hands and feet. We feel hollow and light, suspended in the heavy water like a gas bubble that needs to be burped.

The water seems to be inhaling us, until we are a part of it, made of water, made of lake. We sink a little deeper.

We are numb even when we see Britney's pink hand pointing, and in the depths below us, we see two yellow dots, like a pair of sequins, darting toward us from the center of the lake. It is only when they are close enough that we see their largeness, the hooded eyes, that we scream and our mouths fill with foulness. We flap and somehow our bodies rise, we feel hot sun hit the parts of our backs that break through the sticky water. Eddie grabs our bra straps and hauls us free of the water before shoving us gently back on the grass. Jody is the last one pulled out, and she is quiet, examining her fingers like she does not recognize them, like they have turned a different color.

The rest of us crouch in a row on the bank, dry-heaving and coughing. We rub our arms with spit, trying to erase the lake from us. We shiver and unfamiliar bumps protrude all over our skin.

Eddie stands over us, shaking his head, glaring at us. He looks exactly like our mothers do when they call us brutes. We bristle, curl over our soft bellies, and mutter bad words under our breath.

"You were watching?" he says. "You just sat back and watched while your friend almost drowned?"

He says it in a way like he still has faith in us. Our eyes dance madly. The transition is too quick. He stares at us like he knows us, when we have just convinced ourselves we do not exist. We have no lines prepared.

We look for a savior, a cue card, and Mia is there. She bends over Eddie and imitates his expression of motherly judgment. So we do the worst thing. We laugh. The laugh tastes so bitter it makes us spit. It is cruel because the want inside us is so pure, our jealousy so lethal, our shame so absolute. Eddie looks at all of us but his eyes settle longest on

Christian, who laughs the hardest. He keeps laughing even after we stop. He sounds like a crazy person and Britney has to slap him on the back to shut him up. Then Eddie turns away like he does not know us.

He bends toward Leila. He scoops her up in his long arms. Leila leans her head against his shoulder, and we imagine the warmth of his skin, the steady beat of his heart. We shiver thinking of it, the lake still cold in our bones.

"We're going home," he says. He looks at Mia. "You win. Sammy's yours."

We watch them leave. We are so close to following them. We imagine the triumph of their walk, the applause echoing from the balconies when they return to the apartments, Leila waving the plane ticket as our mothers chant, "Eddie Suarez! Eddie Suarez! Eddie Suarez!"

"Staying or going?" asks Mia.

We stare at her, at ourselves in her sunglasses. Our wet hair sticks to our cheeks.

She reaches over and grabs her backpack, pulls out a bulbous bottle of perfume. She circles us, spraying us with a pink mist. It stings our eyes and the bites on our feet, makes us cough. She appears again as the mist clears, sniffing.

"Still stink," she says. "Wanna come to my house? We can go to Stone's and use his pool."

We do not know what to say. Now that Leila is gone we do not know who is meant to speak.

"Sure," says Christian.

"Sounds good," says Britney.

"Okay," says Jody.

"Cool," says Isabel.

"Yes, please," says Hazel.

"Okay, I think I got it," says Mia.

"Can we see Sammy's house?" says Britney. We kick her but she does not stop. "How about your brother? Is he home?"

Mia picks up Britney's hand and tucks in her fingers until she finds the thumbnail painted Margarita Madness, Mia's shade from three days before.

"I thought I was the one you girls liked," she says, wriggling Britney's thumb.

We look at her. We somehow know this is the last day we will ever paint our nails like her, ever scour the shelves at the pharmacy for her messages. We are no longer sure she is in control of her own mystery.

"Can we have some gum?" says Britney. Mia gives her a single stick and Britney passes it along with each of us taking a tiny bite. Then we stick out our tongues and wag them like synchronized tails.

"You girls sure are creepy," says Mia. She laughs loudly. We snap the gum inside our lips and stare at her until she stops.

LEILA

t's the night before my wedding and I'm thinking about feet.

At all the restaurants I've worked in, we used to perform party tricks after shifts, to help move along the closing tasks. I've seen a hundred waitresses perform their routines. I've seen double handsprings, yogic headstands, wiggling ears, and tongues tied up like flowers. I've seen one girl who picked up a lemon and took a bite out of it like it was an apple. Everyone has something to set themself apart.

I had a few different routines myself.

I could walk the width of a restaurant on my toe bones. I could hold a lighter flame to the callus on my heel and leave it there for a whole minute.

These displays made everyone uncomfortable. I liked to force them all into silence, even the chefs. I felt like a gladiator in ancient Rome, with this impressive show of might. It always sent everyone home afterward.

"Why would you do that to yourself?" I remember the lemon-eating girl saying. Her voice was laced with a judgment faked as concern.

I shrugged.

Why did I strengthen my feet every day over those summers, walking continuously over white-hot sidewalks until I could put out flames with my soles?

I look around the hotel room. Tomorrow, I will be

getting married in a gazebo by a chlorinated pond in the lobby, a body of water that, the event lady proudly told me, "Doesn't have a living thing in it, so there's no worrying if you've got kids or dogs on the guest list." I hate this city, this hotel, and this room, but I feel safer hating things than trying to love them. Everything in here is a different shade of green. The furniture is wicker. On the wall is an oil painting of an alligator. The glass base of the lamp is full of shells, gold MADE IN CHINA stickers glinting among the plastic curves. It is quiet now but there are remnants of the girls everywhere across the room, lipsticked tissues, chewing gum foil, emery boards, nail polish remover pads. They've all gone down to the bar. I was surprised at how many of them turned up for my wedding. We've sat around all day, drinking margaritas, competing over the strength of our memories, most of which don't include me.

I go into the bathroom and look at myself in the mirror. I can tell it's been cleaned with antibacterial spray instead of window cleaner because I have cleaned a thousand restaurant mirrors. There are white scummy lines crisscrossing my face. I want to tell myself something but I have nothing to say. I'd probably tell myself how pretty I was but prettiness has never gotten me anywhere good.

The millionaire came into my restaurant. He was eating alone. He had peppery hair and was somewhat ageless in the way of very rich men.

"Do you know who that is?" the bartender asked me, polishing frantically.

"No," I said. "Don't tell me or I'll go weird."

I was distracted all shift, filled with sudden determination. I dropped a chocolate mousse spoon into a woman's white-silked lap. I filled a man's wineglass to the rim while distracted by my own face in the low light of the mirrors. I forgot olives for every single table.

I felt his eyes all over me.

While I took his payment, he asked if he could take me for a drink. I said okay. Then he asked me how I judged a man.

"By their feet," I said.

He laughed. "We'll see."

When I looked at the tip he'd left a thousand dollars.

This was our relationship from the start. It was only my mother who said I should take that tip and rip it up under his nose, but she was outnumbered by waitresses telling me I was an idiot, and I needed the money. I had just broken up with a bartender I'd been in love with for five years and now I was stuck with full rent. The bartender was an asshole but he drank a lot and I drank a lot and when we were drunk we were so mean to each other that it seemed like the only honest kind of conversation. All day I indulged in the little kindnesses that kept clocks moving, said, "Have a nice day," "How are you?" "Come again soon." Then over late-night dinners, this boy and I destroyed each other with words so cruel and careful they made a kind of poetry. We sanded each other down until we practically shone. But eventually we were so broken that all it took was one touch of tenderness for him to betray me. It could have happened to me, too, but broken men are much more appealing than broken women. Broken men inspire longing. Broken women are just looking to get kicked further down the drain.

The first night in bed with the millionaire, he rubbed his feet up my legs. He seemed delighted by my body hair. I'd anticipated this rightly. Rich men love the idea that you don't care what they think.

"So?" he said.

I felt nauseous. His feet were as smooth and cold as chicken cutlets.

"They're fine," I said.

"Fine?"

"I don't really judge people on their feet," I said. "I was just being funny."

He laughed. "How do you really judge people then?"

"Money," I said, and he smiled.

I noticed his glass on the bedside table was empty and I took it and made him a perfect drink from his wooden, stocked bar downstairs beneath his mezzanine. I filled a glass of water for myself and drank it. He had a weird deep sink, the kind you might bathe a small animal in. There were different settings on the long faucet neck. Boiling water, ice-cold water, sparkling water. All these clear, effervescent, endless varieties of water. I let the faucet run for a while, idly twisting it, and then I took his drink to him.

Six months later, he asked me to marry him. I said yes immediately.

I liked how quiet he was, how large. He didn't seem to feel the need to share anything with me except his things. He placed endless objects in my hands, flowers, plastic containers of expensive food, handles of trash bags, his expression of quiet expectancy never changing, that obviously I was going to cut the stems of his flowers, plate up his food prettily, take out his trash, but that he was also waiting for me to break this silence and refuse his demands. I never did. We lived in a moment of perfectly poised uncertainty. What were we doing? It seemed neither of us knew, so we could live in the moment forever. We moved around his spacious house. I felt like we were evolved aliens, talking in a new language of silence. Other times I felt like we had become mechanical, like we were living inside his back account. I kept making him drinks, and then I made him dinners, and then I stopped leaving his house altogether.

In bed, he folded his limbs around me. His heart was loud inside him and it never changed pace. I imagined it, cold as one of those pendulums real estate agents have in their offices. I stopped sleeping at night.

I never thought about the bartender, but I thought about the boy in the lake.

The memory of him, the bright, stupid orangeness of him, infected my hard-walled heart. I couldn't shake it. My love for him had been so pure and desperate, like a smudgy gel pen heart. He was the only person I ever loved whom I didn't immediately want to destroy. This confused me, in a way I both never wanted to consider and could not stop thinking about.

I texted the girls to ask about what had happened to him, if anyone knew.

"I heard he's some kind of motivational speaker now," wrote Jody. She sent me a link to a website.

There was a photo of him in a white suit, hands clasped, head bent. He was bald and his head shone brightly.

"Were his eyes always green?" I asked one night, drunk at 3:00 a.m., clasped in the millionaire's tight grasp, trying not to use my elbows too much, my breath so close to the screen that my phone appeared to be sweating.

"Yes!" wrote Hazel, with seven crying-laughing faces.

When the millionaire asked where and when I wanted to get married, I looked at the lake boy's website, at the series of tour dates. The font was bright and asymmetrical. There was a photo of him, his teeth two startling white fences, a speech bubble blown out from the darkness between them: ARE YOU READY TO CHANGE YOUR LIFE? LEARN MY POLICY OF RADICAL HONESTY. Tickets were twenty-five dollars and included a glass of red or white wine and snacks.

"I want to get married on July seventeenth in Florida," I said to the millionaire.

He kissed both my kneecaps and told me to hire a planner and tell him where to sign.

"You're so pretty," I say into the dirty mirror in the hotel room bathroom. I say it in a flat, monotone voice, then pull the ugliest face I can manage, stretching my face into one I don't recognize.

"Wow," says a voice from the tub. "Haven't you been told that enough already?"

I turn and pull the curtain. Kayla is in the tub, her head resting on a bath towel, mascara all around her unwashed face so she looks like a raccoon.

"Your friends took up all the beds with their shit, so I came in here to nap and for some goddamn quiet," she says. "You really can't keep a waitress from a wedding, can you?"

"You could have come in with me," I say.

"No, thanks," she says. "I shared a bed with you for enough years."

I laugh.

"You okay?" she says. "What are you thinking about? How you don't really want to marry this guy? That you want to run away to Mexico with me instead?"

I sit on the toilet, rake my hair with my fingers.

Kayla rolls her eyes.

"Okay, not Mexico," she says. "Don't worry, I won't save you from your rich, miserable life."

I nod. I bite my lip to stop myself telling her about the faucet again.

"I can't believe you could have a wedding in Tahiti and you chose to have it here," she says after a while. "We could be on a beach right now. Instead we're sharing a hotel with twenty girls' volleyball teams."

"Can you come somewhere with me?" I ask.

She gets out of the tub.

We walk along the green plush corridor of the hotel and press the button for the elevator. The hotel is huge and white, with a glass ceiling and a glass elevator designed to look like a birdcage. There are plastic sheets of ivy and flower garlands cascading down the walls, shivering slightly in the constantly circulated air. The balconies are at the front of the rooms instead of the back, and the whole design concept seems to be to create Florida as it would be if its nature could evolve more neatly, and flourish in air conditioning. There is a vast pond full of koi fish running through the lobby, a fountain in its middle three tiers high. There are topiaries cut into the shape of a dolphin, a swordfish, and an alligator surrounding the wedding gazebo. I look at the ceiling as we float down. One of the glass panes is cracked, ruining the illusion that the roof is the sky itself. When we reach the lobby, Kayla heads toward the parking lot but I pull her back, along the pond, past a restaurant where a dozen men in suits look up mechanically from laptops and then back again as we pass, and broad-shouldered girls in sports vests eat bowls of pasta, laughing at their phones. We stop at the doors for Conference Room D. An event poster is stuck to them, the print job slightly off so the lake boy's head looks huge. Kayla looks at it, reads aloud, "Are you ready to change your life?" She pauses.

"Is that—?" she says. She starts laughing. "Is that the kid in my class you were obsessed with? The one who used to torture bugs? I thought he'd be a serial killer by now."

"We all used to torture bugs," I say. "You used to burn them. And people."

"Okay, okay," she says. "I forget you were always sensitive about him."

"I'm not," I say.

"Sorry, not sensitive," she says. "Batshit crazy, I mean."

"I just want to hear what he has to say," I say. "It seemed like a sign or something."

Kayla winces. "You only see signs when you want to," she says. "I'll give you a sign. Marry him, don't marry him. Which one sticks?"

I push past her to open two wooden doors beyond.

•

No one asks to see our tickets, though I have the confirmation ready on my phone. The room is small, the carpet thick and printed with wide red roses. There are several rows of bright-pink chairs, the seats covered in a satiny fabric. Before them is a shiny stage, about a foot off the ground. No one is sitting down. Around the snack table, five people are holding paper plates or cupping food in their palms, taking careful pecks. There are two bald men, a tiny old woman, a middle-aged woman in sunglasses with badly dyed red hair, and a girl, about fifteen. The girl is wearing a sweatshirt as a dress, the hem short and revealing large and tanned legs.

"Howdy," says Kayla, bounding over to the snack table and taking a handful of chili nuts into her palm.

The two bald men look at us and nod nervously. The old woman is holding up a plastic tub of hummus and sniffing it. The girl lifts a hand as if to wave at us, but starts to chew on the end of her sleeve instead. The sleeve is ragged, and wet strings drip between her knuckles.

"You know, he's not even naturally bald," one of the men says excitedly. "He chooses to shave his head, but his hair is actually this thick." He holds up an inch-wide gap between his thumb and forefinger.

"How do you know?" asks the girl.

"He posts videos of him shaving it," he says. "It grows so quick he has to do it every month. He says taking the initiative to shave your head shows a lot of power. It works for women, too, but it's harder for women to pull off, if you don't have a certain level of attractiveness, or a je ne sais quoi."

The other bald man nods sympathetically.

The old woman dips her little finger into the hummus. She holds the tiny creamy mound up to the light.

"He could just be editing the videos, you know," says the girl. "You can do that now. You can make yourself into anybody. Or he was wearing a wig."

The redheaded woman shakes her head. "But, honey, that would interfere with his policy of radical honesty," she says. "That's his whole point. I've told you." She looks around at us. "I've told her," she says.

"Radical honesty?" I ask. I look at the girl, but she does not meet my eyes and instead reaches for a carrot stick.

One of the men answers instead. "He believes in absolute truths," he says. "He only talks if he can one hundred percent believe what he is saying. Even if it's a lie, he makes himself believe it. That's the key to doing well in job interviews. He's started a national movement. There's hundreds of us."

"That's not that many," says the girl. She looks at the man and shrugs. "Sorry, but it's not."

"It's growing," says the man. "Soon there'll be a thousand of us!"

The girl opens her mouth to speak again, but her mother interrupts.

"I'm a realtor," she says. "Before coming to these things, I was making maybe a sale a month, I was about to get canned. Then I start following his advice, the total belief thing, it's like a way of focusing your brain. You make every word you say seem important, even when you're talking about basement access or whatever. People go crazy for it. Mommy's made enough lately that my girl's got a Mini Cooper out of it, haven't you, honey?" She slaps the girl on the shoulder.

The girl nods. "It's red," she says.

"A car to drive the boys crazy!" cries her mother.

The girl winds a finger by her head. "So crazy," she says, her voice flat.

"And I've brought her today so she can learn to be as confident as me, haven't I, honey?" says the woman.

The girl chews on her sweater. "A boy tried to kiss me last week," she says, her voice muffled by her sweatshirt. "But then he told me it was a dare to kiss the fattest girl in the grade." She mocks a sad face.

Her mother lowers her voice to a whisper. "And then she took one of Mommy's special Japanese cooking knives to the homecoming dance," she says.

The girl laughs a little.

"Seems a little overboard," says one of the men.

"She didn't do anything!" says the woman. "She was scared, weren't you, honey?"

The girl nods. "I was only gonna drop it on his foot or something," she says. She raises both her hands in the air. "I swear," she says.

"She's joking!" the woman says, and laughs loudly.

"Ha!" says the old woman.

The two bald men snap chips between their teeth. There is a long pause.

"I made out with that guy once in high school," says Kayla. She bats a hand toward a poster on the wall. She looks complacent, but when she looks at me, there is a glint of victory in her eye.

I stare at her. We all stare at her. The red-haired woman looks furious. The old woman puts the hummus in her mouth, closes her eyes, and smiles. The girl says, "Gross!"

"He hardly moved his lips at all," Kayla says. "It was like kissing a locked door. I wouldn't listen to him if I were you."

"But that's what he says!" cries one of the men. "To live well is to be a door. One must be completely closed or completely open, but it is useless to oscillate between these states."

Kayla rolls her eyes, looks at her watch.

"Wasn't this meant to start by now?" she says. "Where the hell is he, anyway?"

The bald man smiles.

"Sometimes he doesn't come," he says. "He can only come if he's ready to speak the absolute truth, so if he can't, he doesn't. The absolute truth, some days, is silence. Actually, I think I like these ones where he doesn't show up best of all. His words confuse me, but his silence has a wonderful clarity to it." He pauses. "Don't you agree?"

Everyone nods and puts another piece of food in their mouths.

Kayla pulls me away toward the door. "I think that's the sign we were looking for," she says. She waves grandly with her free arm, tips an imaginary hat.

"Good luck with changing your life!" calls the girl behind us as the doors slam. I wait for a second, staring at the lake boy's grinning face on the tacked-up poster. Kayla laughs but I want to cry. I always thought I was a strong person, but I'm just like these people waiting for someone to tell them what to do. I can see the sad gang of us all clustered together like a random carriage on a theme park ride, saved together in the godly light of an overpriced photo. I want to get out. I can feel the fear of a slow track rising up before the first loop, knowing I'm stuck, trapped, locked in. And I can see that the person I thought could help me is just a spotty teenage boy on the side of the track, dreaming his way out of a summer job he'll never leave, waving and smiling at me as I scream to be set free.

The rest of the girls are sitting around two plastic tables by the fountain, two bottles of sparkling wine sticking out of ice buckets before them, their hands clutched around stemmed flutes. Britney wolf whistles when we pass, and Hazel knocks over a glass. Christian hails a waiter. Isabel is looking at her phone. Jody has the baby passed out against her chest.

"I'm just going to lie down for a little while," I say, and Kayla dances off toward the others, who scream in unison at her approach.

I stagger up the stairs to the green hotel room and shuffle open the door. The millionaire is lying on the bed, his eyes closed behind reading glasses, a newspaper placed on his chest like a bib. I shut the door softly behind me, and he opens his eyes at the low click. He doesn't say anything, but he looks at me, and the more he looks, the more alarmed he seems, as though only realizing now that I am not a mystery he will never have to solve, but a person, full and humming with shitty life. I am realizing the same thing about him, and it is not a comfortable sensation. I know his name but in my head he is really only a man in a suit. I could leave him now. I could go downstairs and drink wine with the girls. I can already hear their voices, comforting me, concocting plans that will never be realized, until we approach what lies unsaid between us. And then we will finish our glasses, the bottles, and run back to our dusty lives and the dumb men we have chosen to decorate them. We'll spend our days pretending to be happy and sometimes succeeding. We'll lock the doors at night and make coffee in the morning. We'll take comfort in dogs and children and our own secret brilliance at telling lies.

I don't want to lie any longer. I kick off my shoes, wriggle off my socks. I do not speak, but I take the time to raise up on my toe bones. My spine seems to unfurl. I stagger my way across the room to the bed, windmilling my arms for balance, the pain distinct but manageable, my toes the ugly stumps I designed them to be so long ago, when my decisions still felt true. It is the farthest I've ever managed to walk on them, and I feel the child inside me cheer, but when I approach the millionaire, his eyes are closed, his face at careful peace, determined to avoid my performance. A low flame begins to flicker in my throat. I watch as his eyelids flutter, constructing me as a figment of his imagination, a pleasant and pretty dream. His eyes do not open, even when I bend down so close that my breath bends the fluff at his hairline, and even when, after a long pause, I start to speak a truth as sharp as a knife sent through his foot.

12

We follow Mia along the line of the lake, along the white walls. When we reach the gatehouse, our hearts pump, but the gate man does not raise his capped head. Women in Sammy shirts are poking around beneath the orange trees, stabbing at the branches with long sticks so oranges fall and implode softly on the sidewalk. When we reach the gate, it slides open like a waitress gesturing to a table. Our hearts thump with excitement, though we notice that the spikes on the gates are as sharp as arrowheads. They often turn up in our dreams with heads impaled upon them.

In the two pools by the gatehouse, we see that the shimmering orange bodies we thought were real fish are just painted onto the tile. We are thrilled by this. Then we feel hollow. Is everything we find beautiful fake? We close our eyes until we are through the gate and hear it clang shut behind us like a thrown stone.

Our feet feel soothed by an unfamiliar softness. We wince, thinking the ants have got us again, but when we look our feet are smothered by grass. It is not grass we know, this grass is short and soft, like our baby sisters' hair.

We take a deep breath and raise our eyes. We see the white sidewalk, the first we have ever seen without cracks. There are white signs stuck all along it that read, DO NOT STEP ON THE GRASS OR YOU'LL GET GREEN FEET!

We hop onto the sidewalk.

"They dye it for the realtor pics," says Mia. "It gives you foot zits."

We look at our feet. They are already covered in bright-red nipples from the fire ant bites, and now up to our ankles, our skin has a faint tinge of lime green. We do not want to look at our monster feet on the beautiful sidewalk, so we look up at the houses. At the front of every driveway is a perfectly pruned orange tree, the oranges so big they drag down the branches, the leaves oily with health. The houses are spread out with swathes of perfect yard between them. They are white and bulky with weight. They look like the dogs in the dog show at Thanksgiving, something about them so proud and still.

There is not a single leaf on the sidewalk. There is not one brown slick from picked-up dog poop. No fossilized smack of gum. We can't hear any voices.

We follow Mia down streets of identical mansions. The sheriff's car is parked up on one of the driveways, empty. There is no one else around. We look up at the house. The windows are tinted. Yellow crime scene tape stretches across the driveway, shivering and flapping in the first hint of a breeze. We are surprised when Mia leads us toward the house, but then veers off down an alley beside it, a fenced alley where the grass is yellow and patched with sand. She lifts her long nail to the house as we pass it, and we see a window left open, another strip of crime scene tape draped across it, like the cartoon of a smile.

"That's Sammy's bedroom," says Mia.

We look. We think we see a flash of bed, a white netted canopy hanging above it, the kind we always wanted until Britney got one and realized roaches liked to climb it in the night.

We think we see some glow-in-the-dark stars stuck to the walls.

We think we see an army of origami cranes hung from her ceiling, giant versions of her birthday card confetti, their wings impaled with string.

"Come on," says Mia, ahead of us.

We hurry along the fence, past Sammy's yard. We walk through a clump of slash pine trees, the ground littered with needles. We move away from the big houses and the streets toward the wall. We pass another house, painted hot pink, with a huge glass bubble at the top like the house is blowing a gum pop to the sky. We can only see flashes of the house through the trees, but we can see the steel fence ringing around it, the arrows on top of the bars even sharper than the ones on the gates.

Soon we see a row of smaller white condos, attached straight to the back wall like barnacles. There is no grass, not sharp or soft. There is no shade. Each house has a tiny circular pool built into its driveway. We note the glint of bottles, scraps of poop bags, a few rusting bikes turned upside down, an old mattress propped against the wall, washing hung out on lines, the clothes so dry they seem deformed. We see women in uniforms in the top windows of the condos, but when they see us looking, they drop the blinds shut.

Mia leads us toward the house on the end, right next to where the steel-bar fence begins for the pink house. We notice some of the spears have been severed at the base, creating a crawl space. The hole is netted, but the net is only attached on one side. It flaps a little in the rising wind.

The pool in front of the last condo is teardrop shaped, and only just large enough for the huge pink pool float that houses Mia's mother, a sweaty glass tumbler clutched in her hand. There is a collection of multicolored deck chairs strewn around and facing the pool, with a whole flamboyance of women lying across them, fanning themselves with folded magazines and missing posters, holding their glasses of drink to their foreheads, their swimsuits clashing in color and pattern, a pink-and-green zebra stripe, a purple-and-red leopard print, a sunshine-yellow snakeskin. Beside them, there is a barbecue the size of a small car, a man standing behind it in white shorts and white polo shirt, a spatula in one hand. On the table next to him are bowls of guacamole, a stack of grilled pineapple rings, tortillas, and strings of pulled pork like tangles of our hair.

A radio plays fuzzily. As we get close, we hear Mia's mom's voice lisp out from the speakers, "Have you got what it takes?"

All the women laugh, and one burps prettily.

"Hi, Mother!" calls Mia.

Her mom's face tightens, and she looks around wildly until she sees us. She almost flips over the pool float as she swats her way to the edge of the pool. A woman reaches over and gives her a helpful push. She disembarks, rolling off onto the burning concrete like a pancake onto a plate, all the while keeping her sunglasses furiously focused on Mia.

"You!" she says.

The women sip their drinks and flap their hands faster, talk louder.

"What the fuck did you think you were doing at that audition?" says her mother.

The *fuck* exhilarates us. Our mothers still spell out swear words above our heads.

Her mother lurches toward Mia and holds her shoulders, and we can tell by the way her mom's hands are raised that she is digging her nails in.

"I was just trying to embarrass you, Mommy," says Mia. She smiles with her big white teeth. The women stop pretending to talk. Her mother seems to feel the eyes and the quiet, and she lifts her hands up and starts to stroke Mia's face roughly.

"You can't embarrass Mommy, sweetie," she says. She

snakes an arm around her shoulder and stage whispers. "We can speak to Stone, he'll talk to that woman, she really thought she was something, didn't she?"

The women with the glasses click their tongues and nod. One even shakes her shoulders a little, as if dancing to a familiar song.

"They feel like they have to do something different," she says. "I'm sure that boy is a sweetheart, but how is he going to handle life out there? They'll eat him up." She lowers her voice while somehow making it louder. "Does his mother even speak English?"

Christian wriggles. He pulls up his swim shorts. We creep closer to him, we hold his little fingers, we lean our chins into his shoulders, but we do not say anything. We feel stifled, muffled. Our hearts feel misshapen, huge and limp inside our bodies. Christian moves away from us, but Mia stops him, grabs him by the shoulders and pulls him in front of her. Her mother takes a step back.

"Mother," says Mia, "these kids are from the apartments. We're gonna go swimming at Stone's. Is he back yet?"

"Well, stay awhile," says her mother. She looks at Christian, bends down to meet his face like a large bird. "You want some yummy tacos?"

We do. We feel like we might pass out from hunger and from the brutal light, nausea worming around in our bellies.

We run behind Mia and her mother to the snack table.

We do not look at the man behind the barbecue and instead reach out for handfuls of chips.

"You know, the police have a lead on Sammy," says her mother. We freeze. We realize that all the women are turned toward us, watching us. We look at the snack table. We feel there are rules to it we do not understand. The food is untouched. We notice a fat fly crawling in the guacamole. The pork is piled high and around it there is a moat of brown blood. We look around and see the women laughing, or pretending not to laugh, their eyes asking, Where is she?

We withdraw our hands.

"We're not hungry," we say.

Mia sticks her thumb in the smooth guacamole and licks it off.

"Where is she?" she says, and dips again.

"Who knows?" cries one of the women.

"Who cares?" squawks another, and the women laugh, shake their heads.

"Your little show this morning jogged some memories," says her mother. "Apparently she was always getting herself into trouble, climbing over the wall. They even think that boy's involved. They found a ladder."

She shakes her head.

"Stone will speak to the agent," she says. "But she won't want anyone with a sniff of that baggage."

She takes a sip from her glass and smiles.

"So sad what girls will do to themselves," she says.

"They don't appreciate what they have!"

"Her poor mother!"

"She tried so hard."

"You can't help a girl like that."

"She was safe here."

"You know there was another fire yesterday? Burnt out one of those cute little swan pedal boats. You know the ones you can ride around in the resort lake?"

"Oh, I got the cutest pictures on those!"

"Why in God's name would you burn one of them?"

"Won't be someone from here."

"What a shame."

We cross our arms. We look at the wall and it seems to waver. We imagine white bricks jettisoning free, remote-controlled, aimed and shot directly between our eyes.

"What a shame," we imagine the women saying, as we lie in pools of brown blood and fat flies explore our eyeballs.

"A damn shame!" says Mia, in an exaggerated drawl. "Who would ever run around town setting fires for no reason?"

Mia's mother's face tightens.

She looks at us, then at Christian.

"Aren't you that ladder boy's brother?" she says. "Did you see him last night?"

We use our best escape plan. We maneuver around Christian to hide him.

"We have to pee!" we say, like a battle cry. We run toward the nearest house and through the sliding glass doors,
slamming them shut behind our backs and breathing heav-
ily, though when we look back over our shoulders, the
women are frozen in the hellish light, like the machines
on a ride, waiting to come to life only when we are there to
pass by them.

ISABEL

look in the mirror. I wonder if they have designed the lights in here to make everyone look guilty, or maybe that it is just an accidental bonus of being in a Christianity-themed theme park. I let the water run from the faucet. There is a sign that says, HOT WATER! Someone's written in marker underneath, NOT HOLY. The water steams in the basin. I hold the tip of my pinkie in the stream of boiling water for as long as I can before I break and twist the faucet back to cold. The cold water isn't really cold, this is Florida, the water is the color and temperature of pee. My finger hurts.

My daughter comes out of the cubicle, struggling forward with her overalls around her ankles. She is too old to be so naked, she is a tall six-year-old that my mother is always patting on the ass saying, "Good bones! Good bones!" My daughter is tall enough to reach the faucet. I watch her. She twists it and shoves her whole hand underneath the hot water. She retracts her hand and screams. I am there immediately, shoving her hand beneath the cold, but then I hear my son behind me, another twist, he is too small, how could he even reach? But somehow he does, and they both wail, flinging their burning fists to me for kisses. It feels like I am being lightly punched on both sides of the mouth. "Why would they make the water so hot?" I say, and my kids shut up. I do not normally bother to ask for their opinions and the surprise seems to mute them. I take the opportunity to cover up my daughter. My son proudly shows me his behind. "I pooped!" he says. There is a brown streak down the crease. I grab a paper towel and wipe. With one hand and sheer will, I direct him out of his shorts and turn his underwear inside out. My daughter is examining herself in the mirror with assured pleasure. As soon as his shorts are on, my son runs like a dog let off a leash. "Catch him!" I scream to my daughter. There is only one trash can and it is full. I pull aside the top layer to hide the shitty towel but as I do a bloody pad attaches itself to my palm. My kids run out into the dull February light and I do not even have time to wash my hands before I chase them. I am always chasing my children. I remember feeling chased as a child but I never remember my mother chasing me. Perhaps she did not. Perhaps this is why I am the person I turned out to be.

Florida is ugly in February. The land cannot take an in-decisive light. It needs painfully bright sunlight, a ridicu-lous pink sunset, or a storm showing off. It looks terrible when the sun gets gauzy. The whole state seems to wobble with uncertainty. People drink less and there are more car wrecks. The light fades and the whole place just looks like something about to die. You just want to put it out of its misery and let it sink. A new Florida could start over then. We could stop dumping radioactive waste in the lakes. Stop building things out of Styrofoam so the old ladies in the retirement homes aren't blown away every hurricane. Stop with the alligators being rebranded as therapy dogs.

When I got the gold roll of tickets for this park in the mail, I figured what the hell. Tickets are cheap and God can't be any worse for them than the Ugly Duckling. Plus the park is closing down, no doubt fated to become one of those weird abandoned places where teenagers in expensive sneakers take moody photographs of palmettos squeezing their way through old hot dog stands, egrets riding on carousels flipped on their sides, roller coasters rotting in their bright frames. I wanted to come. I wanted to see this park alive in all its cheap and holy glory. If I'd been here with the girls, I would have found it hilarious, but my kids are too young for jokes. They also don't understand the religious context because I have never taken them to church. They do not understand why I think it is funny to see a man dressed as Jesus smoking a cigarette and eating a doughnut at the same time behind the ticket booth.

I look at the guide again. The theme park is meant to be a perfect replica of Jerusalem, though there is a disclaimer at the base: SIZES NOT EXACT! Christians love exclamation points. We've seen the Wailing Wall, the Garden Tomb, and the Wilderness Tabernacle. We've gone through the Museum of Biblical Antiquities. I look at my watch. It's midday. We've only been here two hours. I was hoping this would take up the entire day. My sense of time is carefully divided since I became a mother. I push activities to their limits so there are fewer chunks of time to deal with after. I drag out the days so the evenings are shorter, though recently my daughter has begun a fierce battle against sleep. She says there is a monster in the house. "It lives in the walls," she says. "I hear it in the drains, in the tub. It likes water." She is an earnest and poetic child. She leaves buckets of water around her bed to satisfy this monster, then forgets and tips them over when she wakes up. Her room stinks of damp. I often prefer my son. He is simpler. He likes to run into things at a very high speed and then cling to me until the pain fades. He could do this all day long, it never bores him, the pain followed by the love. I wonder if he is onto something. He wants to experience the two extremes of life constantly. My daughter is doomed. She wants to understand them.

There is a show starting in five minutes called "The House of Lazarus." I read the guide like I'm trying to sell a roach-laden inland timeshare. I have the highest commission in my office. "A tale of love and resurrection!" I cry, gripping their hands and running madly in the direction of the stage.

There is hardly anyone in the park, and there is only one other family in the audience. The mother and father are in ordinary t-shirts and jeans, but the two children are dressed entirely in Florida regalia, from mouse ears to huge red t-shirts to large foam fingers. There is a teenage boy in Roman attire hovering at the end of our row, a large golden ice chest strapped to his front, which he flips open when he sees my son and daughter, jerking forward so they can see inside, where there are dozens of cheap, store-bought red popsicles.

I buy two to shut them up. They do not seem to feel the cold at all. I shiver. The sky is a gray weight, and the seats are unpleasantly damp. The family in the front row laughs together at something the mother says. I look at the stage. It is small, draped in white sheets held up by two columns, spray-painted gold. I close my eyes and wonder if I can sleep through the whole show, if that will be my spiritual awakening.

A girl begins to sing. There is something weird in her voice. I know it in a way that I cannot say, some underline to the lyrics, something beneath the musical-theater trill.

My children look at me with alarm as I jerk upward, but I push their popsicle sticks back into their mouths.

It is her.

She is playing the sister Mary.

I am terrified she will know me, and I slump down in my seat.

She sings, "He would not have died if you were here!"

She clings to the man playing Jesus. He is plump and gray-haired, but the way she looks at him makes me think she finds him beautiful. I take out my phone to film her, but the image is jerky and horrible, and I quickly lower it again. Her hair is long and I hate it.

She convinces Jesus to resurrect Lazarus in a ballad that finishes with a long belting note that receives a standing ovation from the family in the front row. Then she and the woman playing Martha exit the stage. "I'll be right back," I say to my children. "I have to pee."

I entrust the popsicle boy to watch them with a single stretch of my eyebrow, not wanting to use words in case he will say no. I move along the row, bend under a raggedy red velvet rope that says, STAFF ONLY, and creep around the side of the stage. The scene opens up before me in such a cinematic light that I think I must be dreaming, or in heaven. It is not the first time I have dreamed of Sammy, and she always looks just like this when I do. She and the girl playing Martha are crouched on the sand beneath a palm tree, an assortment of shiny trash scattered around their feet. The sun has made a brief reappearance in the sky as if to frame this exact moment, and they are cast in a pool of summery light. Their heads are bent together, a blanket wrapped around their shoulders, and they both have cigarettes drooping from their lips, leaning over a single blue flame.

I am so happy that I forget not to stare. I will run away. I will leave my children, my mother, my carefully crafted life, anything, anything to be their friend, to sneak a cigarette and laugh in the dull, endless February light.

A cloud races in. The scene is cast in gray. They are not girls. They are women. They look at me and smile. Their faces are carved with lines, their fingers yellow. She reaches her hand to her hairline, and I think that she is going to pull off her face like a mask in a horror movie, revealing a dark and stony skull. But she does not. She pulls off the long wig and rubs at her short, fluffy hair.

"Are we spoiling the miracle for you?" she yells out, and they both laugh until the laughs turn to rattling coughs. I turn around and flee.

I want darkness.

I collect my children, who are sitting on either side of the popsicle boy and close to being indoctrinated. "Come on," I say, and there is some urgency in my voice that makes them follow me although my daughter says indignantly, "I want to know what happens to Laz!"

We walk toward the exit. I let my children run ahead, pretend to look around for them, and then dip away into an exhibit called "The Parting of the Seas." The park is so empty that I am sure there are no kidnappers. I just need one second.

The exhibit is an air-conditioned tunnel between two large fish tanks. The tanks are big but the fish inside are tiny, as small and sick as those I have gotten from the pet store, beautiful fish bred to die for my kids.

I sit on a bench and stare at the water.

I try to cry. I try out a wail. I only manage one thin tear but then I notice a robed man in the darkness. I start to cry genuinely because I'm embarrassed. Humiliation has always been my quickest way to weakness. But when he approaches, his voice is kind. He offers me a gold napkin from a dispenser attached to his rope belt.

"You'd be surprised how many people come to cry here," he says.

I nod. I try to look beautiful and sad and holy.

"Thank you," I say.

"No sweat," he says, and grins. "You wanna see me feed the fish?"

I want to follow him. I want him to lead me out of the tunnel and into the light, or to come toward me on the bench and take my chin between his fingers.

"What's your name?" I ask.

"Moses," he says.

"Mommy! Where were you?" screams my daughter. She and my son run into the tunnel and collapse into my sides, crying extravagantly. I tear the golden napkin in two and wipe their eyes at the same time like a windscreen wiper. Then they curl into my body, little pups expert at forming themselves around the softest parts of my flesh. I am all flesh to them. They would be terrified to think of my bones. I want to show them their mother's skull. Look how hard and cold I really am underneath! I would say. But I do not. I hold them. I kiss their soft, smelly hair. We look together at the perfect blue water in the tank before us. A fish zips back and forth. Another does a long wormy-looking shit. Then Moses's brown hand appears in the bright water, throwing neon-colored fish flakes into the tank. The fish kiss his fingers and he gives us a thumbs-up. My son screams and runs up to the glass, pressing his face against it. My daughter stays near, clinging to me. She is afraid of the water, even behind glass. There is a whirring sound, a fan or a filter waking up, and a stream of bubbles erupts inside the tank. The lights in the tunnel flicker faintly. The man finishes his feeding and retreats somewhere behind the tank. He does not return. We are alone.

"Mommy, I love you," says my daughter. Her lips are red from the popsicle. I lean my head close to her ear.

"Listen," I say. "Do you hear that?"

My son bangs on the glass. "Fish man! Fish man!" he demands. I see my daughter's face tighten. She's listening so hard. She needs to learn not to want to please me so much, I think. She needs to learn that the things I tell her are not always good. She needs to know that some of us took other girls back. Some of us led girls by their hands and closed the door behind them.

The pipes in the walls creak. My son knocks and knocks the weakening glass. There is a smell of cigarette smoke hanging in the air. Outside, a heavy clap of thunder passes over. The lights in the tunnel flicker, then fail. The water is bright but obscured with bubbles, the fish fleeing to the corners of the tank, knocking against the glass.

"What is that?" my daughter says. She raises a finger to the tank, her voice shaking. We wait for the bubbles to clear in the water before us, but I already know what my daughter will see if she looks in the empty tank. I can see it, too, clear as a memory, the outline, dark and sticky, creeping closer, a story I wish she did not have to know. I wrap my arms around her shoulders, hide her face. I watch the water. When I feel her calm against me, soften, convince herself that I am there, that it is nothing but a bad dream, I shove her. I shove her toward the glass. She knocks against it softly. She turns back to me immediately, her face taut with disbelief and fury, but I am behind her, already turning her around. Her eyes widen. "It is not just a dream," I whisper, and I hold her steady as she starts to scream.

t is freezing cold inside the house. We can hear the air pulsing out of the vents, circulating and recirculating, getting staler on each route. We imagine hard packs of ice hidden in the walls.

We take the opportunity to snoop around. We climb on the kitchen surfaces to reach the cabinets, but there are no cookies, only saltine crackers and plain chips. We chew on a few but they are dry as straw. We look in the bathroom. The drawers are full of bottles and we spray ourselves with every perfume we can find. The mirror blurs with mist and breath. We look at our crowded faces. We lean in close to one another. We smell like flowers, but underneath there is the smell of rot.

We think of when we were younger and used to dig beneath the banyan, convinced by our older sisters we would find a dead body there, a girl our age they said had run away. Our mothers laughed and told us not to believe our sisters and their scary stories, but we listened. They stuffed us with details until we took plastic shovels and spoons and our hands to the ground, so afraid and excited that we kept swearing we could smell the body. We dug for days until our sisters stopped laughing to tell us they were liars. Still, we were too obsessed to eat. Our mothers and sisters begged us to stop with the digging but it was too late. They told us the girl had moved to a big white house in a city by the sea, but the story belonged to us by then. They did not control it any longer. And we already believed in horror more than we believed in beauty.

"I think I found the lake boy's room!" says Hazel from outside. We hurry after her and bottleneck in a doorway until Jody pushes ahead and we fall into a new, dark room. It smells like moldy fruit and sweat. We think of trash day, blocked drains, the cloud of soft gray that rises when we empty our mothers' ashtrays. The walls are painted black but badly, like someone has done the whole thing with a marker.

Something falls over and lights up. Christian picks it up and returns it to a bedside table. It is a lamp. The base is a ceramic frog, one webbed hand placed on a frog hip, the other reaching up to hold the shade like an umbrella. The shade is veined and frilled at the edges to resemble a lily pad. The lamp throws a mildewed sheen across the room. We notice bright books arranged in leaning towers. A cardboard box full of plastic water guns and gas cans. The bed is unmade, the comforter rolled into a hump at the foot of it. We see three postcards stuck to the wall, flickering in the dim light. There is one of a girl in a black bikini, a bunny traced out from mud scraped across her stomach, a photo of a frog's tongue catching a fly in mid-air, and a blurry Polaroid of the swan boat on fire on the resort lake, the swan's plastic head peering out of the flames with its painted curve of a smile. We notice a missing poster on the bedside table, the edges burnt black.

"Can I help you?" says the hump on the end of the bed.

We leap back to the center of the room. Christian knocks the frog lamp off the table again. The muddy girl falls off the wall. The lake boy sticks his head above the edge of the comforter. Close up, he has a very wide face, and the comforter mounds around him like a body. His eyes are as green and beautiful as the zit-causing grass.

He does not say anything, but he moves and the comforter falls from around his shoulders. He sits on the edge of the bed, reaching down for a red cup on the floor. We can smell its sweet and harsh smell. It makes us feel nauseous and excited. He sniffs it and drinks. He has a very large Adam's apple like a turkey's wattle.

"It stinks like the lake in here," Britney says, and we laugh loudly. He opens his mouth and we instantly silence.

"I think that's you," he says.

He jerks his head to the bed and Britney goes and sits beside him, knocking aside a pair of balled-up boxers with her hip. She sits very still and very straight, but she takes the time to look at us all, inviting us into the scene in a way Leila did not. We move closer, too, though none of us are brave enough to touch the bed, and we cannot look at the boxers. We kneel on the carpet and put our hands on our knees.

We examine how close he is to Britney so we can tell her later. There is a line the width of a pencil between their legs, hips, elbows, widening only at their necks, between his left and her right ear. If he turns toward her, the end of his nose, and possibly his upper lip, will break the line and touch her, his nose grazing the side of her eye, his lip the puff of her cheek. We feel this space between all of us, and it seems to crackle. It is surely an impossible distance to remain intact but it seems equally impossible to cross. A tension vibrates through us that makes us want to do something terrible, like hit him over the head with the frog lamp, or grab his penis and yank it cleanly off.

We are untouched and we long for touch.

We have talked about the touches we have received already.

A boy swam beneath Jody at Bible camp and she swore she felt something stroke her down there. That night, the boy dipped his fingers in a can of tuna fish and walked around the fire getting the other boys to smell his fingers.

Christian told Britney that he smoked weed with one of Andreas's friends and passed out. He woke up with his head in the boy's lap. The boy had taken off his pants but still had his boxers on. Christian was fully clothed so we did not count it as sex. Why did the boy take his pants off? Christian didn't speak to Britney for a week after she told the rest of us.

Isabel stayed at a beach hotel with her mom and little sisters. She snuck down to the pool at night. There was music. Boys swarmed around her like bees. They gave her sips of vodka in a red cup, tart with lime and sweet with sugar. She woke up hours later alone on a deck chair in the dim fresh light of dawn. Her underwear was gone, and she called us freaking out but we hushed her. "You just took them off to pee," said Jody, and we wanted to believe her so we did.

Jody met a boy at the beach when she was making sand-castles with Hazel and he asked if she wanted to take a walk behind the reeds. They lay down on the sand and the boy started to draw swirls across Jody's stomach. Her mom found them and shrieked and threw sand at the boy's eyes. The boy ran. She told Jody to stay still and slapped her. Then her mom cried and said she hated the beach. It was a red tide and the sand was covered with dead jellyfish.

Leila made out with the class president on the last day of school. He called her every day for a month. Sometimes she let him follow us around but he never said a word to us. On the phone he said he loved her every night. She let us listen if we were quiet, though sometimes Britney pre-tended to fart. Leila said to us that he made her want to vomit but she never missed his call.

Britney met a boy online who said he was a profes-sional surfer in St. Pete. When he told her to get the bus out to see him, she freaked out and said she wasn't thir-teen, she was forty and divorced, and he told her she was a fucking perverted cunt. We enjoyed this and liked to say it to one another. "What's up, you fucking perverted cunt?" We laughed until we got stitches.

Hazel fell in love with an actor so hard that she tried to carve the name of every movie he'd been in into her thighs with a dull steak knife.

Britney takes a breath and turns to the lake boy, but he reaches down and picks up his red cup. She hunches back again.

"Where is Sammy?" he says, after he's swallowed. "I've looked everywhere."

Britney says nothing so we say nothing.

He takes a long searching look at us all, and then he turns his head to Britney. The line between them thins, but does not break. We know his breath will be hot and smell like our mothers'. We watch him watch Britney. He scrolls down her body and we do the same. We take in the tuft of hair at her hairline that she burned after it got stuck in the back of a hairdryer, her damp t-shirt sticking and creasing around the outline of her training bra, her white jean shorts, the light hair on her legs catching the lamplight, the fire ant bites pointy with pus all over her green feet. His look lingers especially long on her white jean shorts. We had all been so jealous when she got them, but we can see that because of the lake they have turned transparent, and through them we can see that Britney has stolen one of her mom's thongs. We cross our legs, place our hands over our own crotches in solidarity.

"Where is she?" he says again.

Bravery leaks out of us. Desire chills into devastation, like wanting to touch something behind locked glass.

He takes another sip from the red cup, then passes it to Britney. She takes a large gulp out of it. It seems to steady her shoulders, and she twists her head to the side to look at him, jerking her arm a little so they would touch if only he did not scrabble in his pocket and pull free a lighter, green with a tessellation of leaves. He starts to flick it on and off along his finger.

"She was supposed to meet me, you know," he says. "I got to her window but it was already open. We were gonna get out of here. I had it all figured out for us. Five minutes later and I hear her mom start screaming."

"She didn't want to go with you," says Britney.

We giggle with what we know.

He flinches then, and his elbow, for one delicious second, connects with Britney's. We feel electric waves ring through our bones.

"She wants to run away," says Britney. "But she wants to do it alone."

He flicks the lighter again, laughs a little, swipes his greasy hair over his face.

"Sammy was scared of being alone," he says.

He lowers the lighter, still lit, toward Britney's hand on her lap. He rests the flame on the top of her middle finger. We look at the finger and the flame.

"I know what Sammy wants more than anyone," he says.

He moves the flame over Britney's finger. She does not flinch. She looks at his face and not the flame. His tongue appears between his teeth when he moves the lighter to her fourth finger, then her pinkie, and we feel the flame like it is a tongue, too. It is a moment when what should be clumsy turns cold. We are frozen, glued as we were the first night we saw him. Our eyes are trained on the flame, on the reddening spots on Britney's pink skin. He moves the lighter from her finger, down her wrist and up to the meaty tip of her elbow, where he lingers too long. She draws a breath in through her teeth and jerks her elbow, poking him in the chest.

"You know, no one's gonna fuck you with your pubes like that," he says.

We feel one small heart break, but we look at one another and in our look is a reminder that we have already lived a hundred heartbreaks. We are foolish and resilient.

We spring into action. Britney swoops down and glugs down the remainder of the red cup while Isabel launches forward and takes the lighter from the lake boy's hand. Jody pockets the photo of the swan boat on fire and Hazel plucks up a bright-pink water gun and a gas can. Christian raises the frog lamp above his head.

"What the fuck?" says the lake boy.

Christian replaces the lamp.

"If you know where she is, why won't you tell us?" he says.

"Girls! Where are you?"

It is our mothers' voices.

•

We look around wildly for the door and launch ourselves toward it. We think that if we can only get out of the room then we can lie about the room, although for the first time, we are not sure if this will work for us. It is the first time we have thought that running might not lead to escape, because we cannot outrun what he said about our pubes. We wonder if there's any escape from things we do not like, except for death. We forget that we do not like to think about death. We think about Britney's dad even though we do not like to think about him. We remember the whistle of the shot last summer, and the way he died on the playground bark. We remember the dark birds that flew directly into the sky above his body. We remember the determined marches of the ants crisscrossing him as we waited for the ambulance, Britney's mom stamping madly to keep them away. We remember our mothers whispering when they thought we were not listening: "Why wouldn't he just do it in the lake? Why make such a show?" This is what we remember when we think about death, when the possibilities of it flap too close, and we have to laugh loudly to scare it away.

So we fling ourselves toward the sliding glass doors. The sun flattens and reshapes us. Our mothers are mixed among the women in their bright swimsuits, and for a second, we have trouble distinguishing them. They turn to us, raising frosted glasses, flapping sarongs, picking at strands of pork.

We huddle close to them. They wrap their arms around us, pinch us, and we hide our faces in their backs. They barely look at us, they seem to register our aliveness and then instantly glaze over.

"Girl goes missing—"

"Why did you run off?"

"What do you think you were doing?"

"Are you crazy?"

"Eddie says you almost drowned Leila."

"You brutes."

"She's such a nice, pretty girl!"

"She won't want to be your friend anymore."

We change our minds and duck away from their hands.

"Sweet little Leila," our mothers say.

Sweet, little, alone! we think.

Our mothers look weird in the Falls Landing sunlight. They usually sleep in the daylight and rise with the shadows. They look smaller and softer in the blaze around Mia's pool, their skin looks thinner, and we can almost see the shape of their skulls beneath, like the wolf tucked inside the grandmother. We see the smudges in their makeup, the lines around their eyes and lips from smiling too hard all their lives. We see the freckles across their chests, the bruises on their legs. We see the dryness of their hair, the scratches on their wrists, the patches of dead skin along their knuckles and palms, the peeling redness of their cuticle beds. We have never seen our mothers in such unforgiving light, or we have never really looked at them. They come toward us but we do not know them here. We dive away from their hands like they are zombies looking to consume us back into their flesh, their lives, ones we have, for better or worse, escaped and instantly forgotten.

"They're safe here," says a woman who has taken over Mia's mother's position on the pink pool float, one fake eyelash loose and hanging over her eye.

"The cops are crawling all over out there," says another on the pool steps, gesturing her hand up and over the wall.

Our mothers look at one another.

They look at the cold glasses in their hands.

They look at the chef behind the barbecue. Hazel and Jody's mom is already over there, whispering to him, her fingers dangling a strand of meat into her throat, feeding herself like she is both mother and baby bird.

"Is that Stone's house?"

"The pink one?"

"Aren't you ladies dancers?" says Mia's mother. She reaches for the radio and swings the dial. Our mothers cannot resist cold drinks, sunshine, the rasp of a fast beat. We see their bones begin to twitch and we are relieved when they release us. We clutch our glasses, squint into the light so we cannot see, so we can pretend we still find our mothers beautiful. We have to pretend this, because if we cannot think of them as beautiful, then we have to admit that neither do we think of them as good. And then what would we be? What is a mother or a daughter who is not beautiful or good? We have never heard such a story and we hope we never will.

"Wanna go swim now?" says Mia.

We look at our mothers, we fix them with stares that are bigger and brighter than theirs. We wait to see if they will claim us.

"Go, go," they say. We watch them begin to dance and disappear. Then we crawl through the flap in the fence, Mia leading us.

CHRISTIAN

stare at myself in the sun visor mirror, enjoying the brief respite of shade it casts over my face. I am parked in front of an enormous glass hotel, so bright that it seems to be projecting a force field. Beyond the parking lot, the interstate curls around itself. There is a gas station marking each point of the compass, broken up only by empty fast-food places, a caravan in one of the lots with plastic chairs set up outside, full of smoking men eating arepas, a radio blasting out cumbia.

It seems sad that someone would leave Florida only to end up in Arizona, where the state has invested in the same shades of terra-cotta paint, the same flat strip malls, the same billboards. Maybe it's the same all over America. I don't know, I don't like to travel too much. I like the smell of my own shit. I'm used to it. I went to New York once, and even in the clubs, everyone was in knots about the ice sheets, the impending apocalypse. I couldn't take them seriously with their shocked and earnest expressions. In high school, our football stadium got carried off in a tornado and took out a whole retirement home. A busboy at work last week told me how his abuelo had laid down for a siesta and a sinkhole opened up right beneath the bed, almost a perfect tunnel down toward the center of the earth. "I yelled down at him," he said while we waited for a six-top's desserts. "The echo sounded like his voice. My mama used to go pray for him every week. Would lie down on her stomach and scream into that hole." He shrugged and picked up a tiramisu. "It's a dog groomer's now, though."

My restaurant got shut down because the pest control guy found termites and evacuated everyone during bottomless brunch. The owner let us drink all the stock in the parking lot, knocking back the fancy whisky, cheering when the men arrived and it only took the daintiest of touches for the chewed walls to fall, for the dining room to be opened to the elements. We watched the onslaught, the chairs and tables bombarded with the shells of raining insects. I had a trial shift set up by that evening, but I couldn't stop thinking about the restaurant, how easily it emptied itself out to start again. I decided to take seven days to destroy my life in the most extravagant way possible. I didn't say goodbye to anyone, not even my mother. Leaving was glorious until I realized there was no one left to talk to about it. The more the reality of solo motels and dives deviated from my fantasy of self-renewal, the more I drank. I drank vodka until my head became clear. Then I filled the void with muddy rum. I stopped in six states over seven nights. I curled over bar tops, the dark kind with sweetheart bartenders who can save your life. I turned my head back and forth, swimming into the gaze of various men. Most flickered their eyes away, but there is always one who can't resist the sight of a wreck. I allowed touch to come dressed in these disguises, often tender, always lonely, and when they left, I unscrewed the smoke detectors and filled the room with ghosts of my own making. Glittery ghosts that whispered, sang old songs in my ears: "You're so beautiful, you should be on TV." I ate large burgers every night, each one topped with a different county delicacy, a corn dog, cheesesteak, pork chili, a large onion ring, tinned pineapple, a brown avocado half, and last night's one, stuffed in the center of an iced chocolate doughnut. It was while eating that one that I looked up and saw Eddie on the TV, on some talk show. He sat in a purple chair. Something about the proportions of the chair were off, it was small, like a chair designed for a twelve-year-old. I wondered if this was some trick they did to make celebrities seem even more godly. He was laughing, a gold cross displayed on his chest. My mother used to say she taught Eddie to love God first and her second, and who could resist a boy who still raised his hands in thanks each night and called his mother every Sunday? I wished I could love them all without resentment. I wished I could sit on a Sunday at my mother's new wood table in the suburbs, and be as happy as I was as a child, curled under the old wobbly Formica, looking at all the mothers' painted toenails. I just want to be able to love simply.

In the car, I have a mini bottle I picked up from the grocery store rattling around on the passenger seat. I haven't eaten. I imagine my stomach and liver looking at me with pleading eyes. "No!" they say. My brain comes along with its fat ass and squashes them both. I drink.

By the time I've convinced myself to get out of the car and go into the hotel, it's midday and all is whiteness. I stagger out, gulping in the stale air. It's not soft like Florida air, it's stinging and electric, like static. Two plastic palms sit on either side of the hotel doors, squatting in beige pots with gold edges. The doors revolve slowly. The movement of the glass and the blinding sunlight make the inside of the hotel look like it is underwater. I can see shadows, bodies, but they are blurry, indistinguishable, could be anybody. I step forward, each step taking time, as my brain and body seem to be two whirling extremes, unpartnered, mutually hateful, and I have to command them to connect. Right leg, left leg. Don't trip. Avoid the plant. The revolving doors seem to be moving extremely quickly, like a carousel. Should I wait for them to slow down, stop, release the passengers, welcome me aboard? I look behind me. A family is waiting, patiently, a nice progressive family, standing a safe distance away but smiling. "Go ahead," says the dad. The kids stare at me. I see myself caught in their gazes. Will this be something odd, some fragment that will glint and dig itself into their dumb soft brains, called up at Thanksgiving whenever their parents want to reminisce about all the wonders they have laid at these brats' feet? "Remember the painted deserts? Remember the Grand Canyon?" And the kids will cry, their mouths full of mashed potato, "Remember that man who was scared of revolving doors?"

I force myself forward with such momentum that I

stumble and bump into the spinning glass panel in front of me. I jerk backward and freeze. The doors freeze with me. I begin to knock on the glass panel. My fist lands politely on my watery, useless reflection, confused at this ruined entrance, spectacular only in the saddest of ways. I vow to drink more to forget this. I think I have made a huge mistake.

She appears. Her voice has the tone of someone used to giving orders. She sounds professionally disappointed. There are other voices scattering, weaker ones, of alarm or disapproval, but these fade beneath hers. Behind the sunlit glass, she wavers in and out of time. Her hair is still blond. Her teeth are still large and white. They will outlive her body by a million years, probably. I have come to confront her, to lay the blame for my life at her feet, but I see our faces caught together in the glass and immediately swoon.

"You have to move forward," she says. "You have to go forward, then the doors will come back on. They're on a sensor."

I take a tentative step. The doors wake up and spin me forward. I lurch out and land, for a brief, surprised second, in her arms. I feel her heartbeat announcing itself before we both look away, embarrassed, staring at the shiny marble floor.

We sit on an empty balcony roped off from the hotel restaurant, which is a dark sports bar vibe. Big TVs, booth tables, tall plastic cups, menus thick as Bibles. The balcony tables are laid with gold tablecloths. There are huge flower centerpieces interspersed with neon-colored feathers, looking like stuffed birds of paradise.

"There's a wedding tomorrow," says Mia, gesturing toward the flowers. She moves to a table to pick up one of the towering vases, but then a young girl comes out behind us and takes it from her. The girl has two puffy buns of black hair, a sweet round face.

"You're too nice to me, honey," says Mia as the girl takes the centerpiece from her arms, in a voice so sick with affection that it makes me want to gag. But the girl seems to believe it. She starts to collect the glasses and cutlery from the table. I imagine her covering breakfast shifts for hungover coworkers, cheerfully offering to clean the fridges, the ice machine. I want to take her in my arms and spill all I know to her, which is not much, although waiting tables probably teaches you more about humanity than any therapist could.

"You sure you won't be more comfortable in the air conditioning?" the girl asks, looking worriedly up at the blue blaze above our heads.

"No," says Mia. The girl looks at her, a surprised tremor running through her features that flows into her tray, a seed of doubt. The glasses clink softly. Mia shakes her head, adopts her false cheerful drawl again as the girl slaps two menus down in front of us.

"I'll come put it through, don't worry," says Mia. "I'll be back in an hour for y'all to take your breaks."

"Don't rush yourself," says the girl. Mia smiles. She pats her hands over her stomach, which I can see now is lightly rounded. I swallow. I am so constipated from all the days of drinking and burger-eating. I am suddenly acutely aware that my stomach is full of dead meat.

Mia maintains her glowing, angelic smile until the glass door slides and clicks shut. When we are alone, the smile vanishes. Out of some instinct, the same I'd probably feel to pedal if chucked onto a bike, or to swim if thrown into the deep end, I take a quick note of her nails. They are bare and bitten, red and raw, similar to my own from years of bartending, the cuticle beds chipped by ice, always burning from fruit juice, sticky with liquor.

"So," she says, "you found me. What do you want?"

With a quick glance inside, she digs in her bag. She pulls out a pack of cigarettes and slides it across the table. "Smoke this so I can have a drag," she says. I resent that she has posed it as an order, not a question, but I have never turned down a free smoke.

I take one and light it. I struggle with the lighter, taking five tries to cause a flame. When I take a drag, I cough like it is my first time. Mia laughs at me. She leans her head forward.

"Put your menu up," she says, and I do, propping it to hide her face. Her chin rests on the table, the top of her body splayed. I look down at her, thrown into a dark unflattering relief by the menu. I pass her the cigarette and she takes a long enough breath that half of it falls away into ash.

"So," she says, "you're still following me around? What do you think?"

I clench my knuckles around the menu, thinking I could simply sweep her off the side of the table. But I take the bait and look at her. She looks like her mother in a way she did not before. Her cheekbones have been lifted to make her face less round. Her chin has been razed to be more pointed. She looks like she has been syphoned back to the bone, like the meat at work when the chefs throw it in the sous-vide machine. She looks ready to be served on a plate and consumed.

I take the cigarette back from her hand, prizing it free from her tight fingers.

"Can I get a drink?" I say.

Mia raises her eyebrows.

"Sure, honey," she says. I hate being called *honey*. "What will it be? Why don't I mix us some Bloody Marys? They do dumbass ones here. You can get a full breakfast in them."

I nod. She flies out of the door. I wonder if she'll come back. I smoke another one of her cigarettes. Without alcohol, I have become disconsolate. I cannot believe I am here but I still cannot speak, bestow forgiveness or ask for it, repent or punish. It is a long and cold five minutes beneath the hot sun, in which every dark truth of my life seems to take the opportunity to tap-dance across my rapidly sober-ing head.

She comes back holding two fluted milkshake glasses full of frothy tomato juice and ice, a skewer in each packed with fat green olives, lemon wedges, and jalapeños. I take a sip and it is so cold and full of salt that I feel like crying, as jolted back into my body as when we used to electrocute ourselves on the wild place fence.

"Good, huh?" says Mia.

I nod, my head bent, almost lapping it up.

"I give it to all my no-hope dawn drunks," she says.

I lift my head.

"You're the one who's just been watching me this whole time. When's it my turn?" She puffs out her lip like a baby, then laughs. She ducks her head behind the menu and lights another cigarette. "What have you come here for? To judge or blame me? Convert me to Jesus or Jehovah? What are you gonna do? Stab me?" She leans over to one of the other tables, picks up a tiny fake-gold fork and tosses it over. I almost expect it to come alive and crawl across the table.

"I didn't do anything to you," she says. "You knew what the deal was, everyone did. Two hundred dollars. You know how many kids did it? It's not my fault he got handsy with your friend and you left her there. And it's not my fault if you came back."

I pick up the fork and start to drum it on the table. Maybe I will stab her eye out with it. I take another cold gulp. I don't want to talk about it. I've never wanted to talk about it and I still don't. I've thought about facing her for years, but there's nothing I want to say. Tomorrow will be the same as today, for both of us. This seems incredibly depressing to me, in the way true things often are.

"You don't paint your nails anymore," I say.

"Nope," she says. She starts talking very fast. "Take that as my penance. Three Hail Mary's every night and shitty nails. Do you know what my mother told me when I was five years old? I'd stuck on some nail stickers and she tore them off because they were straight at the top. 'Sweetie,' she said to me, 'I never want to see you with a square nail. Men hate a square nail.' Then she filed them down until they bled."

I don't believe this story but it's true that her mother was a bitch.

"Did she know?" I ask.

Mia drops the stub of her cigarette onto the table. She coughs, then spits lightly into the ash pile. She tamps down the ash with her thumb and begins to spread it in wider and wider circles, rubbing it hard into the soft grain of the garish tablecloth until I am sure no detergent will be able to extricate it. I think of the poor waitress with the puffs of hair, scrubbing it with a sponge in the sink when everyone else has gone home.

"Of course she knew," she says finally. "I told her the first time. She told me to stop being a drama queen. 'He's 'a very nice man,' she said, 'and he's good to us. You're too young to have a dirty mouth like that.' And she took me to the preacher to get more hands on me."

She quits with the ash, folds the menu. She stuffs her sunglasses into her hair and stares at me.

"I thought my mom was right, you know," she says. She shrugs. "Maybe she was, but I'm not going to be like her." Her eyes are not as dark as I remember. They seem faded, smudged. "I don't want anyone else coming to see me," she says. "Go to the cops if you want to cry, okay?"

She drains her drink, then looks at her watch and stands up. She does not look at me. She slides open the door and calls out. The girl with the buns reappears. Mia gestures without looking around at the table, the pile of dirty ash.

"We've had an accident," she says, and rolls her eyes to make it clear I am to blame. The drawl is gone and she sounds exactly like her mother. "We're going to need to order another cloth for tomorrow on express."

I stand up then.

It is my moment.

I imagine smoke curling across the stage, a cast spotlight, a fur coat dropping from my shoulders to reveal an outfit so stunning I cannot even conjure it.

"I'll pay for it," I say. I almost expect to sing but my voice is a whispery crack. "I'll pay for the tablecloth."

The girl with the buns looks confused. She looks at Mia for guidance. I watch Mia's back, the humps of her shoulders turning taut. Five seconds pass, maybe six, then she turns around and laughs. "Whatever helps you sleep at night, honey," she says, and disappears. I expect her to come back, but it's the girl who brings the card machine. It takes me three cards, but finally one creditor hears the voice of God and allows me this stupid attempt at grace. The girl seems flustered at the palpable awkwardness of the scene, but determined to comfort me in the way of benevolent waitresses. "You seen much of the city?" she says, her voice punchy with cheer as the second card declines. I shake my head as we try the third. She wriggles the machine as if this will make it more amenable to my cause. "Well, you don't need to," she says. "Personally, I think we have the best view in the city right here. Sometimes I drive into work and see this glass tower and it looks like I'm in one of those sci-fi movies—you know the ones where the cars are flying? Sometimes I swear I even feel my wheels breeze right off the ground."

I nod at this unexpected soliloquy, take my receipt. She touches my hand gently with the card machine.

"I'm going home now," I say.

"Well, you have a nice day and get home safe," she says. I follow her into the dark restaurant, keeping my gaze straight ahead until I'm back in the lobby. I buy a bottle of water from the reception desk, then lie down in the back seat of my car with the windows down, waiting to sober up. I fall asleep for a few hours, wake up with a dent in my cheek from the seat belt socket. The heat has let up a little and it feels stunning, the coolness baptismal on my skin. I get back in the driver's seat, ready for the long drive home. An old song comes on the radio, a band I once loved so intensely that I could only equate my love for them with offerings of injury: I'd let him run me over with a garbage truck. I sing along by instinct, some crap about being beautiful. I turn carefully out of the lot. The glass hotel tower looks aflame, every window flickering with pink and orange light. I turn the volume up, harmonizing with the noise of the highway, the growl of rush hour traffic, the monotonous mass of shiny things glinting meekly before the cascading desert, drifting outward in every direction to the horizon line. I take the exit, ready for the chorus, the wind blowing my hair wild. I take a breath so deep I feel it in my belly, and when I let it go, hit that first note loudly and hold it hard, I feel so wonderful that, just for a second, I think that I could lift the whole damn highway free from the ancient, endless sands.

14

As we move away from the condo, the sky seems to come closer, like it wants to lie down around the earth. We hear quiet thunder. The pink house is surrounded by a grove of slash pines. The air smells cool and fresh, the way it does before a big rain. It takes us less than a minute to arrive at the end of the tree line. We expect the house to be neatly centered, but it springs up to the left of the path. There is not a single weed growing. We cannot see one shadow of a separated ant, the skitter of a lone lizard. The driveway is bleached and determinedly dead. We walk up to the door. We do not like the dark doors or the dead whiteness of the driveway, but when we look back toward the trees for comfort, the view is no better. The robotic orderliness of the trees makes them look like an army kept at strict bay. We sense that one clap of the hands or click of the fingers will unleash them, and we imagine them bendily encroaching upon us and the house.

Mia rings the bell. We can hear it echoing inside, as if the sound is hitting against many hard surfaces.

The door opens.

A tall girl stares at us, a lollipop stuck into the side of her cheek so she looks like she is growing a tumor. She looms over us and we feel like dolls frozen in a dollhouse.

She has thick eyebrows and a square face.

She is extremely beautiful. She seems full of bones.

"Is he home?" says Mia. "I brought friends over."

The girl looks slowly from the tops of our hairlines, across the sloping planes of our shoulders, down the lines of our waists, all the way to our toes. We shift to avoid the look but it envelops us.

We should have anticipated it, but we are still shocked when the thunder sneaks up loud and close.

The sky begins to spit pellets of rain.

The girl grunts and opens the door to let us in.

A large staircase grows out of her shoulders like two outstretched arms. A huge glass wall leads out toward the pool, blurry, hidden behind the curtains of rain. The pool is cut down into the earth, so it looks almost a part of it, a miniature and much more beautiful version of the lake.

There is hardly any furniture in the house. We walk across a vast open plane to a kitchen, which appears to have been beamed into the house like a hologram. We crawl onto stools around a kitchen island. We drum our fingers on the slab of veined marble and pretend to look bored.

The house is freezing and we rub our arms.

"He'll be back soon," says the tall girl. Her voice is husky and beautiful, with an accent we have not heard before. We want her to keep talking as soon as she stops.

She turns and opens the fridge. It contains a three-gallon jug of milk, a large murky jar of olives, a ketchup bottle squeezed dry. She takes out the milk, reaches into the freezer for a frosted bottle of vodka. She retrieves a packet of Froot Loops from beneath the sink and a red plastic cereal bowl, the kind we have at home, with a straw built into the side for sucking the last of the milk. We relax a little at the innocent sight of the bowl. The girl fills it with bright loops. She lays her lollipop by the sink, leaving a sticky red residue. We watch as she lifts the milk and vodka and pours equal amounts over her cereal, then lifts a brown spoon from the sink bed and takes a heaped bite.

We are mesmerized by her. Her eyes are pale blue.

"You want some cereal?" she says, her mouth full of rainbow mulch.

"No, thanks," says Mia.

We hear a car in the driveway.

The girl looks at us, then cocks her head to one side and grows a grin. She skips away toward the doors. As soon as she is gone, Britney grabs the cereal bowl and takes a long gulp, pink droplets of milk sputtering across the marble island.

"Hey!" the girl shouts, running back. "Don't touch my cereal!"

She slaps Britney around the head, then picks up the bowl and sucks very hard, her eyes bulging. We are so focused on her that we don't even notice him until we see his hand wind around Britney's neck.

"Girls," he says, smiling. He looks like someone returning home to a dinner he will not have to clean up. We do not like his hand on Britney's neck.

"Haven't you learned to share by now?" he says.

We do not like his hand.

"What happened at the audition?" says Mia. "Is she still taking Eddie away?"

He walks around the island. He does not look at the girl, but his hand slides around her waist. She continues eating cereal. We look toward the glass doors, where the rain falls. We feel like we feel when we are in the car wash with our mothers, like we are being briefly held in an unknown universe. We are always calm in the car wash but we are nervous now.

"That woman," he says. "She's nothing, sweetheart. Got her head stuck so far up her own ass—"

He pauses.

"Excuse me," he says. "She doesn't know anything about the industry. You'll do fine out there. I'll take you. It's better for you that way. I'll talk to your mother."

"I don't want her to come," says Mia. He smiles, opens the fridge with one hand, the other still clutching the girl.

"Sweetheart," he says, "can't you go to the grocery store?"

The girl smiles, her teeth coated in chewed-up cereal. We giggle.

"What's that?" he says. "Funny?"

The girl swallows. She lifts her spoon and flies it toward his lips like we play airplane with our baby sisters. He drops his jaw and the girl shoves in the spoon. We sneak our hands over to one another's knees, and one of us must squeeze Mia because she looks at us like she hates our guts.

"Chill," she says.

We lower our eyes and stare hard at the marble.

He knocks his knuckles on it.

"Italian," he says. "Calacatta."

"Cala-what-a?" says Britney, in a loud Italian accent, and we laugh so hard we almost scream.

He looks at us, confused, then laughs, too, but we do not like his laugh and we stop and look at him. We know this can enrage people and we hope to enrage him. We understand rage. But his face does not shift, he looks entirely unaffected by us. We turn quiet and still.

"I go watch television," says the girl. She disappears with her bowl. He does not look after her. He leans his arms on the marble so his big head is below ours. He looks up at us.

"You go watch television?" he says in a weird accent, a bad imitation of the girl, like a villain in a TV movie.

We are lost on where to look. We do not want to look at him. Mia seems to forgive us and starts to pet us. She reaches out, strokes our knees, tucks our hair behind our ears.

"No, they want to stay," she says. "Aren't they pretty?"

He smiles. He looks out of the window at the rain.

"No swimming," he says.

He comes around the island again and puts his hands on the backs of Britney and Mia's necks.

We think of when Hazel fell off a quad bike and had to wear a neck brace for a month. We think of Hazel's dad driving the bike and the beer cans crushed behind them in the red dust.

We think of how Leila's dad once knocked her and Kayla's heads together as a joke, and how her dad cried the hardest because their mom said he'd given them brain damage.

We think of Christian's dad, who we've never met but who sends Christian gifts sometimes, never at his birthday or Christmas, but at weird moments in February, May, October. Beer coasters. A phone charger. Once a packet of golden tomato seeds.

We think of Britney's dad on the playground, and the sound of the birds rising when the shot went through his head. We think of his crumpled body and our mothers feeding us ice cream, playing cartoons loudly so we would not notice the sirens, what they were saying on the phone.

We feel all these feelings at once, together, a dull truth, that no one can ever say what they mean to one another, that words will never come at the right time or in the right way to save us, and that time is only a force edging us along toward our next mistake.

It is best not to think at all, we think.

It is best to float and to follow.

We tuck our greasy hair behind our ears.

Mia wriggles her sunglasses so they fall to the top of her nose and we can see her muddy, lake-colored eyes.

"I love you, girls," she says.

We soften and feel sick.

Sometimes longing and love are equals, but the longing is much more exquisite than the love when it arrives.

We do not want to leave her, leave one another.

We follow her up the stairs.

The corridors are long and punctuated with doors. We hear the sound of a vacuum cleaner, a scrap of music, but we do not see anyone else. We climb a short stairway and arrive in a large dark room. There is a white screen in the center, looming out of the shadows like a square moon. He moves away to turn on a globular spotlight. He swoops it across us and we wince, screw our eyes shut.

No one makes a sound except for Mia. She giggles over and over again, though no one is saying anything to make her laugh. She moves forward and sits in front of the white screen, cross-legged, while he is silent, drifting into the shadows behind the camera.

Then he spins the spotlight and we see the snakes lining the walls.

There are dozens of them nailed between the eyes, their bodies loose and wispy as drying socks. They are pinned neatly in long rows, framed behind glass.

We scream and he and Mia laugh.

"They're dead, dummies," says Mia.

He spits on his thumb and rubs away an invisible mark in front of one of the snake's paralyzed faces. The snake looks permanently to the side, with a manner of great dignity.

"Most are Burmese," he says. "But I took out a couple of natives, too, so it's our secret." He winks. "Amazing creatures," he says. "They see you coming and freeze."

The skins seem to shiver, even though we can see the glass is thick and there is no way the air conditioning is reaching them. They are frozen. We stare, trying to meet their eyes, but he adjusts the light again and the walls darken.

Mia sits brightly in the center of the screen. We feel watched. We have always wanted to be watched. The snakes are our audience, like the audience at the school play, that dark faceless mass we cannot see from the back of the stage, where we wait to be noticed, to be plucked out and into the light.

"Come here," says Mia, and she pats the floor beside her. We think she is talking to us but he is there, too. He looks terrible sitting with his legs crossed.

We sit very still in a circle. All our knees touch. We hate for our knees to touch, we like to leave space for the possibility of touching. We shift to make the circle wider, but he shoves up closer to us.

Mia crawls out of the circle and sits behind him. She starts to massage his shoulders through his polo shirt, balling up her fist then stretching her fingers in the shape of a flower. We knuckle our lips. We want to laugh at his dreamy, stupid expression. She had not told us we would have to touch him. He takes off his shirt and Mia doesn't pause, her hand massages the air for a moment before connecting again, as if there is no difference between his shirt and his skin. There is a distant sound of clicking. We do not like to look at him but we cannot stop.

"Come on," Mia mouths over his shoulder. Britney is the first, she scoots over on her butt, and when she presses her hand into his other shoulder blade, she mouths, "Ewwwwwww."

We laugh silently and mime puking.

His skin feels like raw chicken.

Mia looks embarrassed. We relax a little, thinking of the girl on the wall, the girl falling off the stage, the girl crouched in the shadow of the cars, alone. We look at her and not at him. We keep our hands on the man's back, thinking it will please her, keep her close to us. We look around and our thoughts take on a cool logic. We think of lizards losing their tails, shedding snakes, and we fidget as though we can bust the seams of our skins, too, feel them float softly from us, revealing bodies as hard and thin as bones. We can hear clicking, and we start to count the clicks, thinking every click is another step toward whatever this is being over. We imagine ourselves in reverse, moving backward from the room, backward through the doors and the trees and under the fence, back to our mothers, moving their way through the light, ready to take our hands and move us through the light, too. But we cannot reach our mothers in the light because we are in the dark. Even in our thoughts, they are too far, the house is too large, and we cannot remember where the door is. We know clocks cannot turn backward, anyway. After a while, I look around and realize the others have left me. I am alone and he turns to look at me. It is not a look I like. He looks so scared of me. He looks like he almost hates me, but at the same time I feel like I am indistinct and unreal to him. He looks at me in such a way that I feel I am being created for him. I do not want to be his mirage. I do not want him to make me. I listen to his thoughts. I cannot help it. I realize I am being blamed. He is telling me how powerful I am, how beautiful. He is telling me over and over so loudly that my own thoughts are drowned out. I crawl into a silence deep inside myself where it is cold and dark and safe. A cavernous silence, where his thoughts are pebbles, skipping stones thrown far away. But still, I can hear him. He says it is my hands that lead him, he shows me this even as he holds down my wrists. It is no one's fault, he thinks. It is not my fault you are here. I do not want to be you. I do not want to be you. I do not want to be you. I look around for someone else to be but I am alone and I have always been so scared of being alone.

15

do not want to clutter the room with any more words. I'll just say this.

Imagine for a second there is inside you something like a soul. This soul is like a bowl of still water. It sits, a clean and precious thing, balanced in your chest. The water is cool. Holy. It is entirely itself. It is like water before *water* was a word. Now, imagine a syringe. The vial is brown and, as you look at it, you realize it is full of human shit, the tiniest, foulest amount. And imagine this needle being pressed, slowly, into the skin of your sternum, injected, as you watch helplessly, into this bowl of balanced water. How quickly it spreads and stinks and fouls this cleanest thing at your center. And in seconds the bowl is ruined. And you look at the bowl and feel terrible you were unable to protect it, this precious and fragile and perfect thing. And you recognize the life's work it will take to wash and repair the bowl, and it is not fair, because it is not you who dirtied it. So you tip the bowl over and it breaks. You pretend it does not exist.

But then there are times when a feeling crawls across you. The feeling is all the sadder and truer because you cannot name it. You can live a happy enough life with a broken bowl inside you. But you will always be wanting, a feeling as keen and common to you now as thirst.

16

ast night, we watched when Sammy arrived on the wall. She was early. The sun had not yet set. We trained our binoculars, ready to mark the change in timings, wondering what it meant, but then we saw she was waving. We swung around to see who the wave was for, but there was no one there. She continued to wave and point and then we focused on her mouth and saw it made the shape of our names.

We had not known she knew our names.

We did not know what to do.

She kept calling us, flapping her arms wildly, looking behind her. We left our binoculars and ran down the stairs and across the construction site and around the line of the lake. The sun was bright, the sky was blue. We stood beneath her feet and looked up at her.

"I'm going to jump," she said.

We shook our heads.

"I'm going to," she said.

We shook our heads.

We ran to the show home and kicked the door open. We were surprised at how ugly it was in the light, how much it stank. For the first time in our lives, we wished we were wearing shoes. But we kept going. We knew there were sacrifices to be made for love.

We unhooked the jumper cables that held the tent up

above the mattress, and then we ran back to the wall. We held the tent taut and our arms bulged with determination.

We nodded and she did not pause.

She fell from the wall in a delicate tumble, like a shirt collapsing from a line. The tent zipped through our hands but we gritted our teeth and held it, caught her so that she only skimmed the hot grass.

"I need to hide," she said.

We nodded. We thought.

Cars streamed along the highway.

The show home was full of holes, we'd taken the last remaining cover.

Our still-alive grandmothers would be out on the balconies, watching everything.

We could not keep her too close to the lake.

We knew we had to hide her in the place no one dared to go.

We gave her Leila's hoodie and she slipped it over her head. She instantly looked like one of us. She copied our walks, our loud laughter. We knew then that she had been watching us, too. This was the first love we knew. We felt like mothers. We took her under our arms and led her across the apartments and to the wild place.

We took turns banging the lock with our fists until the rusty catch sparked and unclicked. The grass was so tall and thick that when we pushed it aside we made a gap just large enough for our bodies. As we pushed forward, the grass folded behind us and we could not see the fence or know what direction it was in. We were surrounded by green, by humid breath. We battled our way forward until we bumped into two sick palm trees. We spun around with our arms out to flatten the grass, the sharp blades cutting up our skin.

Sammy sat cross-legged between us as we circled her, making her a nest. We did not mind. She was our baby, sucking her thumb. We were taking care of her. We felt angelic.

We gave her our warm cans of soda, the last of the candy and dusty gum in our pockets.

"You need sugar," we said.

"You need sleep," we said.

We strung the tent between the two palm trees and told her to lie in it like a hammock.

We told her to stay still to fool the snakes.

We tucked some of our pepper sprays beside her.

She stared up at the sky. We looked, too, but there were no clouds to interpret what was going to happen, only empty, endless blue.

"There's something in me," she said.

She drew a circle on her belly with one of our pink pepper sprays.

"Like a baby?" we said.

"Not a baby," she said.

Isabel bent to her knees. She had four babies in her

apartment, two from her mom and two from her mom's new boyfriend. They lay in cradles like reptiles in tanks and Isabel tended to them. She knew everything there was to know about babies.

She tugged up Sammy's t-shirt without asking her if she could.

Her stomach was flat.

Isabel bent her ear toward it, but as soon as her ear touched the skin she jerked backward, like when we let the lighter linger too long between our fingers.

"What is it?" we said.

Isabel shook her head.

"Don't tell anyone," said Sammy. "Tell anyone I'm here and I'll kill you."

"We'll come back when it's safe," we told Sammy.

"They're not going to stop looking," she said.

"We'll think of something," we said.

We turned and battled our way back through the grass.

Before we broke apart and returned to our bedrooms, we asked Isabel again. We were jumpy and knew that at any moment Eddie would descend with his ladder, that maybe Sammy's mother was already screaming at the sight of her empty bed.

"What was it?" we said.

"I don't know," said Isabel. "But it flapped."

JODY

leave the room and follow the sound of a television. I open a door and see the tall girl, a cluster of bones on a huge white couch in the shape of an *L*. The television throws blue clouds of light across the otherwise dark room. I hear the thunder rolling uselessly across the house. It is suddenly funny to me that people are afraid of thunder, as though noise alone can do any damage.

"Are you okay?" asks the tall girl. I nod. The other girls are in similar positions around the room, on the white fur rug, leaning against the couch, or curled up close together, clutching cushions.

We watch television. I can see my face reflected on the screen, a moony phantom. I look dead. I hold a cushion up to my eyes to hide.

It is a show I know because my grandmother used to like watching it in the dead middle of the afternoon. It's a reality show where a rich person pretends to be poor for a week. They set the rich person challenges like guessing how much things cost and a host follows them around, repeating what the rich person says and then laughing at them.

"Ten dollars for a carton of milk?"

"Ten dollars?"

"You're kidding me!"

A rich boy in a fur coat is trying to do a poor family's grocery shopping on their weekly budget. He has thirty minutes. There is a countdown in the corner of the screen telling how much time he has left. He runs around the grocery store shrieking and knocking things over. "This is so stressful!" he cries. He lies down in the aisle. "I give up!" he says, then immediately gets up again. The tall girl laughs loudly and I copy her, but as soon as I laugh she turns to me fiercely, her face flat and still, so I stop.

"These are your friends?" she says.

I don't look at the other girls. I shrug. I look at her and with my look I try to communicate that we know the same things and are the same. She turns away. She reaches out with one long arm to where Hazel sits on the rug, crying quietly. She hits Hazel beneath the chin.

"Ouch!" says Christian, and throws a cushion at the tall girl. It misses and lands softly on the fur rug. The tall girl picks up her cereal bowl and takes a long bubbling slurp from the milky remains.

"Bad girl," she says.

On the television, the rich boy tries to add things up on a giant, hot-pink calculator. The presenter stands with the cashier. They both shake their heads and laugh indulgently. They begin to count down from ten.

"Stupid boy," says the tall girl. She flings her bitten nails toward the television, then sticks the middle one in her mouth and gnaws on it.

"What's your name?" Christian asks.

"Elena," she says.

"Where are you from?" Christian asks.

"Estonia," she says.

"Do you like it better here or there?" says Isabel. Her voice squeaks.

Elena laughs. "Here, I am a supermodel," she says. She waves her arm around the dark room. "At the American modeling agency!"

She laughs so we laugh, too. Then she throws her cereal bowl toward the television. Neither object seems affected at all. The bowl lands upside down and a ripple of pink milk spreads and mats the white fur rug.

"Six months ago, I was a factory girl making matches," she says. "And look at me now."

"Seriously?" says Hazel, between sniffs.

"No," says Elena. "I was at the mall. Just like you. Eating a fucking hot dog."

She looks back at the screen. The light scrolls across her. The rich boy fits everything into his budget. He laughs with the presenter and the cashier about how ignorant he was of the cost of things, how much he can buy for so little. "This has been so inspiring!" he says. They show him climbing the stairs to a private plane, the poor family waving on the tarmac, the wind blowing their hair wild. "He was funny," says one of the kids, sadly.

"Do you take classes at Star Search?" asks Christian.

"My mom works there," says Britney.

"We're all gonna go to L.A.," says Hazel.

Elena doesn't say anything. After a minute of silence, Isabel crawls over the rug and picks up the cereal bowl. Then she crawls back to the couch, rising only to her knees to hand it back to Elena. She takes it without looking at Isabel. There is a whip of lightning outside the window and the lights flicker and the television screen turns dark.

"Damnit," says Elena, jabbing at a thin silver remote.

The lights come back on.

The television screen turns a brilliant white, and the image seems to scatter into a million pieces before coalescing again. When it comes together, I am shocked. I shift closer to the screen. I can see the white house with the tinted glass, untouched except for Sammy's bedroom window, burnt up to a dark hole.

A news anchor stands before the window, holding a fat microphone and an umbrella blowing inward from the wind. Rain spatters the camera and the image is repetitively obscured as a hand wipes it apologetically with a cloth.

"We understand a suspect is already in custody!" screams the woman over the sound of the storm. "There is no known motivation for the arson and it is believed to be unrelated to the search for Samantha."

A fire engine flashes its disco lights on the street. Men stand around holding long yellow hoses, the sky full of smoke and rain. I run to the window and pluck the blind. Dark fingers of smoke creep across the window screen.

I look back at the television.

Women approach to stand in front of the window, their arms squid-like around one another. "Where is she?" they sing.

"Mom?" says Hazel.

I grab her hand and we all run from the room, along the rows of doors. I do not slow my pace even when I am lost, turning in circles, every door the same. I continue to run until I see the white staircase and the white floor, and the doors fly open at my touch.

The sky outside is heavy and swirling, like the storm is some escaped creature the sky is wrestling back inside. I run across the driveway and through the silvery pine trees, dull in the new dark. The rain falls. I take one look up at the pink and quiet house, and then I never look back. Not that it matters. I will never need to look at that house again to see it.

I slip first through the flapping fence. Mia's driveway is empty. The deck chairs are abandoned, the rain pooling in craters in the guacamole bowl, the pink strands of pork floating on the plate, the pineapple rings bloated and soggy. The barbecue is propped open and hissing as the rain hits the coals. The pool is overflowing, water lapping over the sides in waves, the pink float beached on the concrete.

I run until I see our mothers, gathered by the fallen fence, arms wrapped around one another, the fence gesturing toward Sammy's window like a flat hand. They thread together to form a wall but I stand on my toes to see over their shoulders.

Sammy's window is gone, replaced by that burnt and black hole.

Her room is robbed of color. Ash and smoke hangs around us in the air. I rub two smudges onto Hazel's cheeks like battle stripes. Christian sticks out his tongue and a clump lands on it like a snowflake. Sammy's parents clutch each other on their front stoop. The church women are all gathered on their driveway, swaying in the wind. I can see some boys from the apartments. The lake boy stands alone, farther away toward the gate, a large plastic water gun stuck deep in the back pocket of his jeans.

I can't deny the beauty of it. I think of the stripe on his thumb, the slick of the match, the click of the lighter. I understand it is the way he wants to show his love, but I see his love means less than I thought. She has traveled so far from this room. And if it was anyone's, it was her match to light.

My mother plucks something from the grass. Hazel makes a little whimpering sound beside me, and I hold her shoulder to stop her from running over. My mother staggers to the woman with the microphone and shoves up close to her. She sways a little. The woman looks shocked, but she is clinging to the umbrella when a gust of wind knocks her off-balance, and my mother takes the chance to grab the microphone from her hand. My mother holds up a strip of notebook paper to the camera.

There is a rustle as the voices in the crowd rise up, curious. "Where is she?" they call.

"Gone swimming," my mother reads, in a clear and grand voice. The note is written in bubble letters with a smiley face at the end. The crowd is quiet, except for Sammy's mother, who rises up on the steps and releases a long, low scream. There is a pause. The women seem to respect the scream, they wait to confirm it is over, and then, one by one, they add their own. The lady with the microphone winces, and begins to drag her hand across her throat, mouthing, "Cut!" fiercely to the man behind the camera.

I look at the broken glass in front of Sammy's window, the burnt patch of earth the size of a grave or a door. I gesture to the girls and run toward the trash beside the condos, making a sprint for the wall. I can faintly hear my mother screaming, and as I listen I can tell her voice forms the shape of my name, but I have disappeared and I know she cannot see me anymore.

I have seen Sammy jump onto the wall so many times that I know on instinct where to find the trampoline. At the end of the line of condos, there is a thick bush of bougainvillea growing over and among an assortment of trash, a rusting bed frame, a few beer kegs, a filing cabinet. At the base of the flowery nest, there is a circular, empty tunnel. I shimmy to my stomach and slide through. My hands are full of dry leaves, and a few surprised bugs run for cover down the collar of my t-shirt. The girls behind me spit and pull on my ankles.

"Move!"

"Stop!"

"Hurry!"

I stop when my head bumps against a short stone wall. I reach up blindly, feel a ledge, and heave myself up onto a raised and abandoned balcony, the trampoline standing on top of it like a forgotten temple to a story no one knows. I am the first. I leap onto the trampoline, building up a bounce. I stare at the wall and it looks like an evil white grin stretched across the landscape, and I launch up with a cry.

I miss. I miss again and again. The wall is slippery and it takes me twenty-six times, but finally I am there, straddling the top of the wall. The storm inflates the sky. I knock my leg against the ladder and see Leila, waiting for us. I launch down and she almost falls over with the strength of my hug, and then the others are there, over and over, collapsing into one another.

Lightning forks the highway and fractures the great dark glass of the lake. The thunder sweeps across the water. I am bruised and grazed, my skin is sticky and stings. Christian, Isabel, and Britney grab the ladder, scuttling with it toward the lake bank. They feed it to the water, slipping it down its throat.

•

My breath is smooth, my heartbeat steady. I seem to blow toward the wild place. The only human sound in the storm comes from a couple in the show home, screaming with laughter and sex, but I do not stop to look through the window. I run around the lake, past the apartment blocks, our windows warm with yellow light. The lake is a frenzy of glitter as the rain hits it. I reach the wild place, tug at the sparking fence, wincing as the jolts weave through my fingers. The tall grass beyond is beaded with shiny black drops of rain. I jam the gate open and slip in quickly to the green world. The sound of the storm is muffled. I march forward, and shadows slide around me, but it is only the girls following me and their carousel of shadows.

"Sammy!" I call. "Sammy!"

"She's here," Christian cries.

I follow his voice that is so like her voice.

He huddles by her head, stroking her shorn beautiful hair.

She is shivering. Her lips are white, her skin flaky with sunburn.

We gather around her.

She groans.

"My stomach is killing me," she says.

She throws her head back.

"What the fuck," she says.

She raises her knees.

"Get it out of me," she says.

I look at Isabel. Isabel shrugs. She looks at her watch as if it contains an answer.

I roll my eyes. I push through the grass and look between Sammy's legs, through the loose material of her shorts. There is a path of sticky black blood trickling down her legs.

"Is it your period?" I say.

The others gather around to look, too.

Britney winces.

"Ew," she says.

"What should we do?" says Christian.

"Oh, fuck," says Sammy. She closes her eyes. Drops of sweat form on her forehead, mixing with the rain.

"She's not gonna die, is she?" says Christian.

"We shouldn't have left her," I say.

"That was your idea!" says Britney.

"No, it wasn't!" says Leila.

"Does anyone have any water?" says Isabel.

Hazel starts to cry again.

"Shut up!" screams Sammy, and we do, even Hazel.

Sammy jerks.

She reaches down and pulls off her pajama shorts, and, in a sudden lurch, she springs out of the tent. Her skin cracks from burns as she moves. She sits down on the flattened grass with her knees raised. She rests her chin in the cove between them. She stares at me with a steady cool gaze that I have never forgotten.

"You look," she says. "And don't even think about telling me what it is."

I do not want to look but I know I have to.

I squint into the tent hammock, into her pajama shorts.

I expect to see a black and sticky bird, bald and beakless.

I expect the bird that flew into the air when Britney's dad fell.

I expect it to tell me who the heads on the gate in my dreams are.

I expect it to pluck my heart free and show me the black slug Leila coughed up from the lake.

But it is not a bird.

It is a silly, tiny, baby stone.

It is a pebble.

It is misshapen, and smooth, and coated in blood.

There is nothing special about it.

It is not scary.

It makes me mad.

I spit on it roughly and wipe it with the tent until it is clean, but there is nothing more to say about it or to see.

"How am I gonna get out of here?" says Sammy.

I stare at the stone as if daring it to move. I go to put it in my pocket, but Britney stops me, puts it in hers. She fidgets slightly, and I stare at the outline of the stone against her leg, but no one says anything.

"I don't want anyone to know," says Sammy.

"I have an idea," I say. "To distract them."

I clean Sammy's pajama shorts as best as I can in the wet grass but she won't wear them.

"You can't run away with no pants on," I say.

Sammy rolls her eyes.

"I'm not wearing them," she says. "I'd rather be naked on the Greyhound. I'd rather lie down and die."

Hazel surprises me by being the first to offer her own shorts.

Sammy watches her suspiciously, but pulls them on.

She does not thank her.

Hazel grimaces as she pulls on Sammy's bloody ones. She stands with her legs wide apart, but I can see the watery slicks where her thighs rub.

A black snake with yellow hyphens on its back undulates around our feet.

I can hear wings in the grasses, and I think of wasps creeping out of giant ears.

I know we do not have much time.

I tell Hazel to run and bring another pair of our mothers' rhinestone flip-flops. I stuff some cash into Sammy's hoodie pocket.

"We'll distract them," I say.

Christian stays with her, so she is not noticeable and alone.

The rest of us fight our way back through the grass.

I clutch the fence to give myself a brief shock, and tumble back into the world. The rain has been pushed out from the sky by the sunset.

I run toward the white tent.

The construction site is full of mothers.

They look like women who have been reborn, their faces are bright and dry and smiling.

The air is cool and stunning.

The pink light falls and makes everyone look beautiful.

The walls of the white tent have been rolled up to allow all the women to sit. They ripple out across the boundaries of the tent, across the grass and beams of the construction site. They form a huge circle. More and more women keep appearing, from between the white walls, the apartments, the highway.

I run toward Sammy's dad. I know he is the one I can lie to. I cannot look at her crying mother. I know I will tell her the truth if she asks.

He is humped over on the small stage, like a broken angel.

We whisper together in his ears, we fly our little fingers toward the water.

"One at a time," he says, but I know it is best for us to speak together. He only needs to catch a few words.

"Lake," Britney says.

"Monster," Isabel says.

"Gone swimming," I say.

He looks over across the sea of bent and praying heads, toward the bright lake and its huge pink belly.

He shakes his head.

"No," he says.

"Yes," I say.

"Please," he says.

"We saw her," I say.

I think of Britney's dad, the squawk of the bird and the blood on the bark.

"I'm sorry," I say. We scatter and disappear into the crowd.

I find my mother and lean against her hip.

She strokes my hair, kisses my head. She does not ask where I have been, she does not want to know. I forgive her. I do not want to know her, either, not really.

I find the other girls and wait.

The boats arrive quickly. Men descend on the lake with their tools, fishing rods and long spikes baited with chicken carcasses.

The sheriff leads the way, looking proud and dismissive, his time, finally, to shine.

The sky seems to be trying to burn itself out.

Younger girls, little sisters and cousins, bring me offerings, coffee, slurps of beer, french fries. Their little faces are bright with hope, like they expect me to favor them.

I am bored.

I flick a lighter over the little girls' fingers.

I smoke the cigarette stubs that are scattered around the show home steps and do not share them. I throw the final orange darts through the show home window where the sleeping couple lies dreaming, oblivious, roofless and exposed to the elements.

I resent their lack of shame.

The men in the boats dart and soar across the lake.

I imagine Sammy at the bus station, ascending the steps and disappearing to the back like she used to on the school bus.

I wonder what she sees in the roof.

I imagine the darkness streaming past her window, a distant city laid out before her like a smashed glass of light.

I have been chasing that feeling my whole life.

The beams of the men's flashlights skate across the lake's still surface.

The air blurs with the last of the day's heat, the sun elegantly bowing beneath the lake. I can see every pink particle in the air. Sammy's dad murmurs into his megaphone.

"Where is she?"

"Where is she?"

"Where is she?"

The women repeat his words, they sing it like a song, the words as meaningless as wind.

Britney screams.

We look at her. We gather around to hide her from the mothers. She whacks her thigh, wriggling and writhing. She pulls off her sticky shorts and struggles away from them up the grass, pulling down the hem of her polo shirt to cover herself.

The stone creeps out of her pocket like a slug.

I can see it has tiny teeth.

Britney slaps her thigh, at the round, black bruise blossoming there. I crawl over to her. We spit and swipe and swat at the mark to see if we can rub it off, but it only seems to get darker the more we touch it.

When I look back, the stone is gone, disappeared into the water.

One man on the lake whistles over the women's where-is-she song.

The whistle is piercing, and it seems to poke holes in the song. I watch him carefully.

He zigzags across the lake, then stops near the shore, close enough that I can see all the details of him even though I do not want to.

He stops whistling.

He yells out to the other boats. Sammy's dad lowers his megaphone.

The mothers creep closer, they touch our shoulders, stroke our hair. They are silent. Everyone is watching the man in the boat.

Sammy's mother strides out into the water, her pink t-shirt puddling the surface. She clings to the lake as if she thinks she can hold on to it.

Sammy's father drops the megaphone to the grass. He closes his eyes.

The whistling man's arms turn taut.

The other men zoom toward him. They hop into his boat and grab the line. Together they pull up what it is that shakes the black water, that tugs the line and the boat down toward its still and dark room.

The men pull and pull.

I watch the monster rise out of the water, the lake falling from around its body.

It is no monster.

It is a small and oil-dark creature, with growths all along its skin that look like tumors. It looks dead.

"Should we take the kids inside?" a mother asks faintly. Mothers grab the littlest ones, cover their eyes, and spin them roughly away from the water.

The creature is far too small to contain a girl, but the whistling man seems excited by the capture. He wraps the creature's jaw in one hand. In the other, he holds a hunting knife up to the last glowing light, and he does not hesitate. He slices a deep cut through the creature's white belly. A curtain of blood sweeps out into the boat.

"Don't look!" cry the mothers.

The creature looks so small and so dead, but its eyes are still open, still yellow. Close your eyes! I think. Give up! But it stares and stares at the man with the knife.

The man seems to see the eyes, too, because even though the thing was obviously mostly dead when they hauled it out, he continues to stab it until blood runs out in all directions, like the creature is being drained.

The men around him creep quietly back to their boats.

The whistling man is alone with the creature and the knife.

He is covered in waxy blood.

He looks embarrassed, like he does not know what to do with the knife.

Eventually, he drops it.

The creature's eyes turn the color of milk.

"Is it dead?" asks a little sister.

"Was that a gator?" asks a little brother.

"That was the weirdest thing I've ever seen," says a sister.

"Weirder than your face?" says a brother.

"That definitely didn't have any girl in it," says a sister.

"Maybe it had cancer," says a brother.

"It was, like, deformed," says a sister.

"That's a mean word!" says a brother.

"Mommy, is it dead?" asks the littlest girl again. She starts to cry.

Her mother swoops her up, holds the girl to her chest.

"It's just sleeping," her mother says.

Another little girl who is almost as large as me folds her arms.

"That thing is not sleeping," she says.

Another mother threads two hands around the bigger girl's neck. The girl's neck is so thin that the mother's fingers seem to touch at their tips.

"No way is that thing sleeping," the girl says.

"You hush," says the mother. "You'll scare your sister."

The boats make their way back to shore. Phones begin to ring everywhere. Sammy's mom and dad fold themselves into the sheriff's car and it screeches away.

The creature is tossed into the back of a truck bed and covered up with a tarp.

"Let's go home," say the mothers.

They grab the nearest girl, pulling us by the arms.

I do not move. I shake my arm free.

I stare at the surface of the lake.

"Say good night," say the mothers.

My eyes are heavy but I pry them open with my hands.

"It's just sleeping," they say.

I watch the water move.

No one else seems to see.

The mothers retreat, the little girls and boys retreat.

They drift past me. They talk about dinner, drinks, sleep, babies, money.

I cannot stand it.

I cannot let them leave.

"It isn't sleeping!" I scream.

And then the lake bursts into flame.

They all turn back to watch.

Curtains of fire rise from the mud that wraps around the lake's edges. The smell of burning fertilizer is unbearable. We hold our shirts over our noses. No one speaks or screams or even breathes. The flames skate across the sticky surface of the lake. Smoke rises into the air and hovers above the water. It seems like it could blow in any direction, toward us or away, but I am not afraid of the lake anymore.

Sometimes the world deserves a burning.

ACKNOWLEDGMENTS

Thank you to Emmie Francis, Kendall Storey, and everyone at Catapult and Faber for making this book a reality. Thank you to my agent, Harriet Moore, for believing in it since the beginning.

Thank you to Maura Dooley, Jack Underwood, and everyone at Goldsmiths for the early support, and to Danny Denton and the Stinging Fly for the encouragement to keep writing. Thank you to the staff at the Fallow Deer, Llewelyn's, and Eat Vietnam, and to the students at Jewellery Quarter Academy. Thank you to Alex.

Thank you to my thirteen-year-old gang: Kelli, Alex, Raquel, Celeste, Carolyn, Carina, and Justine. Thank you to Laura and Paige. Thank you to Jon, Livia, Charlie, Emily Rayfield, Emily Cooper, Amy, Molly, Helen, Oscar, and Su.

Thanks to my family: Dani, Dom, Dex, Finn, Freya, Emme, and Deacon. And thanks especially to my mum and dad.

DIZZ TATE grew up in Florida and lives in London. She has had her short stories published in *Granta*, *The Stinging Fly*, *Dazed*, and *No Tokens Journal*, among other publications. She was longlisted for the Sunday Times Audible Short Story Award in 2020 and won the Bristol Short Story Prize in 2019. *Brutes* is her first novel.